MISSFITS FASTPITCH

www.jstuddard.com

Missfits Fastpitch

Copyright ©2012 by Jody Studdard

Cover Design: Jody Studdard

ISBN-10: 148956831X
ISBN-13: 978-1489568311

For Jennie Finch
Softball Superstar

Chapter 1

I hate judges. They're always so old, and grumpy, and arrogant. They sit up there on their stand, in their fancy black robes, peering down at you through thick, dark-rimmed glasses. Judge Wilson is the worst. He's completely bald, with huge bags under his eyes, and he looks like he's a hundred years old, maybe more. And worst of all, he's always in a bad mood, at least when I'm in his courtroom.

But then again, I shouldn't be in his courtroom.

Especially since it's the third time in the past year.

But at least I'm not alone. Misery loves company, right? Three of my best friends (Madison Johnson, Kaya Suzuki, and Jennie Miller) are sitting next to me, facing the same fate as me. Once again, we're at Judge Wilson's mercy. This time, however, I don't think we're going to see much mercy.

Judge Wilson lowers the file he was reading, removes his glasses, and turns to our defense attorney, who sits directly to my right. "Counsel," he says. "Would you like to explain how these young ladies ended up in my courtroom again?"

He puts special emphasis on the word 'again.'

Our defense attorney, a man in his late twenties named James Kingsley, rises to his feet to respond to Judge Wilson's question.

5

"Your honor," he says. "This was all a misunderstanding. My clients —"

"A misunderstanding?" Judge Wilson interrupts. "Four young ladies, all fifteen, were at a party drinking alcohol. How is that a misunderstanding?"

"The police report isn't completely clear," James says. "Many portions are vague and confusing. There's no clear evidence my clients were consuming alcohol."

"It seems pretty clear to me," Judge Wilson says. "Regardless, it's irrelevant. At the last hearing, I ordered them to stay away from parties or any environment where alcohol is present. Like I do in all cases with underage alcohol consumption."

There is a long, awkward silence as both men wait for the other to say something. I fully expect James to come forward with something more in our defense, since he's a great attorney and he did a wonderful job at our past hearings. Both times, we got little more than a warning, a scowl, and a few hours of community service. But this time, I can tell he's struggling, and he really doesn't know what to say, which is unusual since he's usually so articulate.

Finally Judge Wilson breaks the silence.

"Here at the Justice Center," he says, "I see these cases every day. Minors in possession. It happens. It's not good, but it happens. But I find this case especially troubling, since I've now seen these particular ladies three times. Correct me if I'm wrong, counsel, but at the last hearing, and at the one before that, didn't you assure me this type of thing wasn't going to happen again?"

James clears his throat, then adjusts his tic. He's really sweating now. And for good reason. It's true.

At the last hearing, he assured Judge Wilson we had cleaned up our act and he would never see us again.

"I did," he says.

"Then why are these young ladies back in my courtroom?" Judge Wilson asks.

"Girls will be girls," James says. "But I assure you, your honor, I've discussed this problem with my clients, and they assure me this is the last time."

Judge Wilson laughs. "I've heard that before," he says. "Correct me if I'm wrong, counsel, but at the last hearing, I gave your clients a thirty day sentence, correct?"

"Correct," James says.

"And I suspended all thirty of those days on numerous conditions, including no repeat offenses within six months. Correct?"

"Correct," James says.

At this point, I don't really know what the two men are talking about (James explained the term 'suspended sentence' to me once but I forget what it means), but I know it isn't good. Especially since James's face is getting red. He clearly knows where Judge Wilson is heading with this line of questioning and doesn't like it.

"So," Judge Wilson says, "why shouldn't I give these ladies the full thirty day sentence, in the juvenile detention center, beginning immediately? Perhaps that would take care of the problem once and for all. Or at least for thirty days. In the detention center, the ladies won't have any access to parties or alcohol."

For a brief second, I think I'm going to pass out right there on the spot. Thirty days in the detention center (in case you don't know, the detention center is our county's version of a jail for teens)? What am I going to do in the detention center for thirty days? It's a nightmare of epic proportions.

"The detention center may be exactly what these ladies need," Judge Wilson says. "They'll finally get some discipline and some appropriate supervision."

He puts special emphasis on the word 'appropriate.'

He shoots a nasty glance at our parents, most of which are sitting in the rows behind us. I turn slightly toward my dad, who is sitting in the front row to my right, and see he has an awkward, embarrassed, angry look on his face.

I don't really want to spend thirty days in the detention center, but after seeing the expression on my dad's face, it may not be such a bad idea after all. I may need the protection. If I'm allowed to go home after this hearing, I'll likely face the death penalty. Or something worse, if there is anything worse than the death penalty.

"Thirty days is so harsh," James says. "Perhaps your honor will consider a shorter sentence. A week would be plenty to teach the ladies a lesson."

Judge Wilson scowls, but much to my surprise he actually considers James's proposal. "Perhaps," he says. "A week in the detention center, without their phones, should do it."

At that, I can't help myself. "What?" I ask. "We don't get our phones when we're in the detention center?"

Judge Wilson shakes his head.

I can't believe what I just heard. An entire week without a cell phone? That's worse than the death penalty. Now I might as well head home and face the wrath of my dad.

"That's not fair," I tell Judge Wilson. "That's cruel and unusual."

James immediately signals for me to be silent, and I wait anxiously, nervously, fully expecting Judge Wilson to give me a nasty reprimand, but he doesn't.

"Perhaps," he says. "And it's definitely not my preferred way of handling cases like these. You four probably think I'm this old, terrible, grumpy judge, but I assure you, Miss Parker, I take no pleasure in sending young ladies to the detention center. But I can't let this problem continue. So I need a solution. What's it going to be?"

For the next couple of minutes, you can hear a pin drop in the courtroom. The only sound is Judge Wilson's law clerk, who is organizing files to one side. I try my hardest to think of something, but nothing comes to mind. I turn to James, knowing he's by far the smartest one of all of us, and I pray he can think of something. But much to my dismay, he sits there, completely speechless.

"There must be something the four of you can do," Judge Wilson says, "to keep yourselves out of trouble. Don't you have any hobbies?"

We look at each other, but no one says anything. At one point, Madison opens her mouth, and I think she's about to say something, but then she has second thoughts and decides to remain silent. Kaya and Jennie just sit there, clearly too afraid to say anything.

Hobbies? To be honest, the closest thing I have to a hobby is collecting friends on Facebook. For awhile, when I was young, I collected dolls, but that came to an end years ago.

"What about sports?" Judge Wilson asks. "A lot of kids these days stay out of trouble by playing sports. Do you four play any sports?"

9

Once again, there is silence. None of us play any sports.

Somehow, I muster the courage to speak. "We used to play softball," I say. "Back in Little League. But that was years ago."

"I love softball," Judge Wilson says. "My granddaughter plays for a select team called the Washington Wildcats. Have you heard of it?"

Unfortunately, we haven't, so after exchanging several quick glances, we all shake our heads.

"Regardless," Judge Wilson says. "You may be on to something, Miss Parker. I tend to think most youth these days get in trouble because they're bored and have nothing better to do. So they turn to shoplifting, and drinking, and sometimes drugs. I tend to think these things wouldn't happen nearly as often if kids had a way to occupy their time and stay busy. So maybe that's what we should do with the four of you. Instead of sending you to the detention center, maybe I should find a way to keep you busy, so busy you don't have time to get in trouble. And softball is great for that. Especially select softball, like my granddaughter plays. With all of the practices, and the tournaments, and the workout sessions, you'll be busy most of the week. The more I think about it, the more I like it. So that's what I'm going to do. You ladies are going to form a softball team, a select team, and practice at least three times a week, with at least two tournaments a month. And we'll schedule a review hearing in six weeks so I can see how you're doing."

"Sir," James says. "I don't know much about softball, especially select softball, but I imagine forming a team must have some expense involved, tournament fees and equipment and insurance, among other things. None of the ladies have much money."

Judge Wilson rubs his chin. "I'll authorize the use of some funds from the court's registry," he says. "Not a lot, but enough to cover the basics."

"That's most generous," James says, "but the ladies will also need a coach, and possibly a manager of some sort, to keep things in line. I'm not convinced four teenage girls can run a team by themselves."

"I agree," Judge Wilson says. "That's where you come in, Mr. Kingsley. You're going to be their coach."

James's eyes get big. He clearly cannot believe what he just heard. "Sir," he says. "With all due respect, I don't know anything about softball."

Judge Wilson smiles. "I remember," he says, "you used to be quite an athlete back in the day, counsel. Didn't you play on a local team that won state?"

"That was years ago," James says. "Before I went to college, and to law school. I haven't touched a baseball in years."

"You'll shake the rust off," Judge Wilson says.

"Your honor," James says. "Baseball and softball are related, but completely different, sports. I don't know anything about softball."

Judge Wilson shrugs. "That's not a problem," he says. "What do you do when you get a legal case you know little about?"

"Like all attorneys," James says, "I do some research."

"Exactly," Judge Wilson says. "So do a little research. Teach yourself how to coach softball, and help me keep these ladies out of trouble."

James hesitates for a long second, weighing his options carefully, before speaking again. "With all due respect," he says. "I have no desire to coach a softball team."

"Then I'll order you to do it," Judge Wilson says.

James's eyes get large. "Sir," he says. "I seriously doubt the court has the authority to make an order of that nature."

Judge Wilson glares at him. "Like always," he says. "You can appeal my decision, counsel. But you're going to be in front of me next week, handling another case, and the week after that, and the week after that, handling others. Do you want to be on my bad side?"

I raise an eyebrow. To be honest, I've never seen James speechless before. But right now, he is. He's actually beyond speechless. He's completely dumbfounded. His face is red and his eyes have glossed over.

"So it's settled," Judge Wilson says. "My sentence is as follows: you ladies will form a softball team, you will have three practices a week, and at least two tournaments a month. We'll schedule a review hearing in six weeks, to see how things are progressing and make adjustments as necessary. From there we will decide what we are going to do next. In the meantime, you four will stay out of trouble and have no contact with alcohol whatsoever. Understood?"

We all look at each other, but none of us are too excited about it. A softball team? None of us have played softball since Little League, and never at the select level. I used to be a pretty good pitcher, and I had a nice fastball, but I'm not certain I remember how to throw one now.

"I'm not too excited about it," I say.

"Me, neither," Madison says.

Judge Wilson grows stern. "You have two options," he says. "Softball, as I've proposed, or thirty days in the detention center. With no phones. It's your choice. What's it going to be?"

Our answer is swift and unanimous.

"Softball," we say.

Chapter 2

My problems don't end when I leave the courtroom. If anything, they intensify. My parents are furious and embarrassed, and they ground me for a month. They don't even wait 'til we get home to punish me, and my sentence is handed down to me in the car during the drive from the courthouse. I'm grounded for a month, which basically means I have to come straight home from school every day, and I'm not allowed to hang out with Madison, Jennie, Kaya, or any of my other friends (except at Judge Wilson's court-ordered softball practices), and my allowance is suspended, too, indefinitely. I still have to do my chores, but I don't get paid for it. That sucks. Oh well. I'm used to having no money, so screw it. The one good thing, however, is my parents decide I can keep my cell phone, and to be honest that's all that really matters to me, so thank goodness for that.

So it's a pretty boring night to say the least. I spend most of the evening in my bedroom, pretty much trying to avoid everyone else, which isn't difficult since my dad isn't really in a talkative mood, and my mom is so upset she can barely look at me. Her face is still bright red, and it shows no signs of returning to its normal color. My younger brother Steven asks my parents how things went, but they tell him they're not in the mood to talk about it, and they don't want him to bring it up again, and they send him to his room. He shoots me a nasty look as he heads down the hall, and clearly he's not too happy with me, either.

My only companion is my cat, Mr. Snugalot. Mr. Snugalot is a big, gray tom, with bright green eyes and super long whiskers (I wish my eyelashes were like that), and I've had him since he was a kitten. Like most animals, he loves me regardless of what I've done, so he spends most of the night in my room with me, sleeping on the end of the bed. I rub him under the chin, which is something he really likes. He tips his head back and purrs loudly.

After awhile, I tire of petting him, so I head out to the garage.

"Where are you going, young lady?" my dad asks as I pass his den. He's in there, like usual, sitting at his desk. He says he's working on something from the office, but like usual he's really just checking ESPN to see how the Mariners did tonight.

"I'm going out to the garage," I say. "I need to round up my softball stuff for tomorrow's practice."

He nods, so I take that as approval and head out to the garage. I find my old softball bag in one corner, buried under a pile of other things, including two bags of beauty bark and another bag of fertilizer. Man that stuff stinks. My softball bag has been laying there since my last Little League game so many years ago. It's dark blue, with white straps, and it actually is still in okay shape, despite the fact it's covered with beauty bark (one of those bags must have a leak in it). I pull it free and do my best to wipe it off, and the minute I get a good look at it, it brings back a load of fond memories. I played Little League for three years, and it was really fun. Madison,

Jennie, and Kaya were on the same team as me, as were several of our friends at school (we went to Whittier Elementary back then), and our coach was a man named Tyson Jones. He was one of the other girl's dads, but I don't really remember which one. We weren't very good the first year we played (I couldn't throw a strike to save my life), but we made a lot of improvement during the next two years (especially me), and we ended up being a force to be reckoned with. We won the district title when Kaya hit an inside-the-park home run. At one point, we all fantasized about winning the state championship and going to the Little League world championship.

But then, for whatever reason, we lost interest, and we moved on to other things. I think Madison played for one more year after Jennie, Kaya, and I quit the team, but I'm not sure. I'll have to double check with her.

Anyway, I unzip the bag, which is not an easy task, and the zipper sticks at two different places, but eventually I get it all of the way open and look inside. It's crammed full of stuff, including my old bat, mitt, batting gloves, and Little League uniform (whoops, I think I was supposed to return that). Oh well, too late now. My bat and mitt are still in decent shape, but my batting gloves look terrible, and they're missing two fingers. For a brief minute, I'm tempted to head inside and ask my dad if he'll buy me a new pair, but then I decide this isn't really a good time to ask him for anything, so I nix the idea. I grab my uniform and take it back to my room, where I try it on, but as expected it's way too small, and I can barely get it over my head. The pants are a little better, I can at least get them on, but boy are they tight.

A few minutes later, I get text messages from Kaya, Madison, and Jennie, and they basically relay the same story as mine. They're all grounded, for varying lengths of time. Kaya, like me, got a month, Madison got six weeks (that sucks), and Jennie got two weeks (her parents have always been pretty lax, and her dad is a push-over, so it figures). We talk about various things, and then eventually Madison brings up Judge Wilson's ruling.

"I thought we were headed to the detention center for sure," she texts.

"Me, too," I text.

"Me 3," Jennie texts.

"I can't believe he put us on a softball team," Kaya texts. "It's going to be so lame."

"Tell me about it," I say. "There are a million other things I'd rather be doing with my time. Shopping, for instance."

"So true," Madison texts.

"I guess the one good thing," Jennie texts, "is that it'll get us out of here for awhile. I'm sick of my bedroom already."

"Tell me about it," Jennie texts.

"Do you guys think James will be a good coach?" I text.

"I doubt it," Madison texts. "He didn't seem too happy about the whole thing. He didn't even say goodbye to us after the hearing. He just packed up his briefcase and left."

"Yeah," I text. "His face was pretty red."

"Nothing we can do," Jennie texts. "What's done is done. Now I guess we just have to deal with it."

"I guess so," I text.

With that, our conversation comes to an end. Madison mentions something about a cute boy in her math class, but I'm not really much in the mood to talk about cute boys right now (which is actually quite unusual, 'cause I'm always in the mood to talk about cute boys), so I toss my phone on my desk, give Mr. Snugalot a quick rub under the chin, and head into the bathroom to take a shower.

Chapter 3

Our first practice is today, and it's a complete joke. There are only four of us, and James is a half hour late, and when he does show up he's in a bad mood and doesn't even bring any equipment.

"What kind of coach," I ask, "shows up late to a practice?"

"And what kind of coach," Jennie asks, "doesn't bring any equipment? How can we practice without any equipment?"

"You'll get your equipment," James says, "when I get around to getting it. Some of us have jobs, remember? I don't get to sit around all day surfing the internet on my iPhone like the four of you."

"Whatever," I say.

We all stand there for several minutes, waiting for someone else to say something. Finally, I can't take it any longer.

"Aren't you going to do something?" I ask. "You're the coach."

"Like what?" he asks.

"Like teach us to play softball," Jennie says.

James shrugs. "I don't know how to play softball," he says. "And I thought you all played before. Little League or something. So you should know how to play, right?"

"It's been a long time," I say.

"Well then," James says. "Go out on the field and do something."

Not knowing what else to do, we head out onto the field. Since James didn't bring any equipment, we're forced to make do with the small amount of things we brought, which are mostly old, worn out gloves, bats, and balls from our Little League days. We form two lines and start tossing the balls back and forth. In the meantime, James sits down in the bleachers, pulls out his cell phone, and starts surfing the internet.

"What kind of coach," Jennie asks, "surfs the internet during a practice?"

"I never wanted to be your coach at all," James says. "So I'm just putting in my time. Sooner or later, Judge Wilson will realize this whole thing is a fiasco and put an end to it, then we can all return to our normal lives."

We're all pretty surprised by James's attitude. To be honest, none of us wants to play softball, either, but at least we're going through the motions. James, on the other hand, is totally against it.

But then again, I can't blame him. He's an attorney, in his upper twenties, and he probably has better things to do with his time than spend it with a bunch of teenage girls. He's probably got a girlfriend, or a wife, who he'd rather spend his evenings with. In addition, unlike us, he never did anything wrong, but he's getting punished anyway, and it's pretty ironic really, since all he tried to do was his job, which was defend us. So I guess I can understand why he's so sore about it.

At the same time, however, it's still surprising. When we met James in the past, in his office and at the courthouse, he was always so friendly and cordial.

Right now, however, he is the exact opposite — standoffish and outright hostile.

So we continue warming up for about twenty minutes, and then we head out onto the infield, where we do our best to imitate some of the drills we remember from Little League. We take turns hitting grounders to each other, and one of us plays first base, so we can practice our throws across the infield. It's a disaster. It's been so long since we played we are all super rusty. One of my throws slips out of my hand and flies across the nearby street. It misses a parked car by less than a foot. Another hits a dumpster in the nearby parking lot and sends a stray cat fleeing for its life.

James looks up and shakes his head. Clearly, he thinks this is hopeless.

He's probably right.

Not knowing what else to do, we decide to run a few laps around the field, since our Little League coaches always made us run laps during practices, but we immediately regret the decision. We're all in miserable shape. Even Kaya, who is the smallest and thinnest of the four of us, is huffing and puffing within minutes.

It dawns on me I haven't formally introduced everyone yet, so I guess I should take a few minutes to do so.

Madison is about my height (5'6") and like me, she's pretty thin, maybe even a little on the lanky side. Unlike me, however, she has bleach blonde hair (don't tell her, but I think she uses way too much). She has brown eyes and teeth that are almost as bright as her hair. She's a nice girl, but she's always had a little bit of an edge to her, and you definitely don't want to make her mad or you'll feel the wrath for sure.

Kaya is the shortest of the four of us, but not by much. She has gorgeous, jet-black hair and sparkling brown eyes. All of the guys at school think she's the hottest thing around, so she always has a boyfriend or two. She has a spunky personality and her nickname, at least when she was little, was 'Firecracker.'

Jennie is a little taller than Kaya, but not quite as tall as Madison and me, and she has brown hair, bright blue eyes, and chipmunk cheeks, with large dimples on each. We've teased her about her cheeks for as long as I can remember. They're actually quite pretty, but we give her a hard time anyway. She is one of the nicest, calmest people I've ever met, and I can't remember the last time I saw her get mad.

When we finally finish the last lap (we have to walk the final hundred yards), we plop down on the bleachers around James and take a much needed water break.

"What should we call our team?" Madison asks.

"What do you mean?" I ask.

"We've gotta have a name, right?" Madison says. "All teams have a name."

"I think," Jennie says, "we should be called the Panthers."

"Why Panthers?" I ask.

Jennie shrugs. "I don't know," she says. "I just like it. Either that or Tigers."

"Tigers is too common," Madison says. "We need something new. Something different."

"Like what?" I ask.

"How about Angels?" Madison asks.

James looks up from his cell phone and snickers. "Angels?" he says. "If you four were Angels, we wouldn't be here right now."

I don't really like his attitude, but he has a point. We're definitely not angels. Angels don't go to parties and drink alcohol.

"What about Devils?" I ask.

"That's definitely more appropriate," James says.

"What about Misfits?" Madison asks. "It's kinda like Devils, but not quite so evil. And it does describe us well, since, well, we're a bunch of misfits."

We all nod. Misfits does seem pretty appropriate. But it's still not quite right.

"It's too plain," Kaya says. "Let's add something to it. Something to spice it up. Like Lady Misfits."

"Lady Misfits?" Madison asks.

"Yeah," Kaya says. "A lot of softball teams add the word 'Lady' before their name. Like the Lady Sharks. And the Lady Hawks."

"And the Lady Cats," Jennie says.

"I still think it's not quite right," I say. "We need something a little different. Something unique. Something other teams haven't done before. So we'll really stand out."

"Like what?" Kaya asks.

At first, I'm not certain how to respond, so I say nothing. There is a long silence as we sit there, trying desperately to think of something. After what seems like an eternity, something comes to mind.

"What about Missfits?" I ask. "With two Ss."

"It already has two Ss," Madison says.

"I mean in the first part of the word," I say. "Like Miss, as in a girl."

"That is pretty creative," Kaya says.

"Sounds corny to me," James says.

23

We ignore him.

"I like it," I say.

"Me, too," Jennie says.

"Whatever," James says. "It's your team, so you can call it whatever you want."

I turn to the girls.

"So is it official?" I ask. "Are we the Missfits?"

Everyone nods. "We're the Missfits," we say.

Ten minutes later, we call it good and head for home.

Chapter 4

We have the worst coach ever. Today, James shows up at practice, and he's late again (by an hour this time). But I'll at least give him some credit, since he brought some equipment with him, including a couple of new bats he bought using the money Judge Wilson allocated for us from the court's registry (I don't really know what the court registry is, but I guess it's a bank account or something similar). The bats are really nice, and we instantly start using them to do some batting drills, and once again James sits in the bleachers surfing the web as we practice.

"Aren't you ever going to do anything?" I ask.

"I am doing something," he says. "I'm downloading some music from iTunes. Have you guys heard the new song from Five Finger Death Punch?"

We shake our heads. None of us have heard of Five Finger Death Punch before. He plays us a clip, and to be honest, it sounds like someone went ballistic on a set of drums.

We spend an hour doing various batting drills, then do a little infield practice, but to be honest we aren't much better than the day before. As always, several of our throws are wild, and one of Madison's throws actually knocks James's phone out of his hands. It doesn't break it, but it makes him mad anyway, and he orders us to go and run some laps.

25

We're not really too excited about running laps, and I'm still sore from the day before, but we all laugh as we take off. It's kinda ironic, and I doubt James even realizes it, but by making us run some laps, he actually acted like a coach for the first time. Who knows, maybe he has some potential after all.

But, to be honest, I doubt it.

Chapter 5

Today is a first. James actually shows up to practice on time, and he has a girl with him. Like the rest of us, she is fifteen, and she is tall and thin, with deep, brown hair and matching brown eyes. She is wearing sweatpants and a sweatshirt and carries a softball bag over one shoulder.

"Ladies," he says. "This is Aubree Tanner. Miss Tanner decided to go on a little shoplifting spree last week, so Judge Wilson ordered her onto the team with the rest of you."

"Do you like softball?" I ask.

"No," she says. "But I didn't have a choice. Judge Wilson said it was this or the detention center for thirty days. I said I'd take the detention center, but then he said I couldn't have my phone. So I changed my mind right quick."

We all laugh. Her story sounds very familiar to us.

"Welcome to the team," I say. Then I turn to James. "This brings up a good point. We need more girls. Five isn't enough for a team. Is Judge Wilson going to send some more?"

"Maybe on occasion," James says. "But I'm not certain."

"Then what are we going to do?" I ask. "We can't play games with only five girls. We need at least nine."

"Twelve is ideal," Kaya says. "Just in case we get tired or injured."

James shrugs. "Don't look at me," he says. "This is your team. If you need more girls, then you're going to have to get them yourselves."

"Where are we going to get softball players?" Madison asks. "They don't grow on trees."

"Why don't we text some of our old teammates," Kaya says, "from Little League, and see if they want to play. Like Payton and Zoe."

"And Hannah," I add. "She may be willing to play. She was really good, back in the day."

No one has any other ideas, so we give it a try. It takes us quite awhile to think of everyone on our old team, and most of us are pretty sure none of them will be interested, but we are pleasantly surprised. We actually get four volunteers, so we' now up to nine girls. It's the bare minimum needed to field a team, and if anyone gets hurt or misses a game we're in big trouble, but at least it's a start.

Chapter 6

Today we work on positions. We pretty much just fall back on our Little League days and reclaim the spots we played back then. Madison goes to first, Kaya to second, Jennie to third, Aubree catches, and our Little League teammates (which we recruited by text the day before) take shortstop and the outfield positions.

That leaves me to do the pitching. Back in our Little League days, I was actually a pretty good pitcher, and I led us to the state playoffs one year. But that was a long time ago, and boy am I rusty now. I can barely remember how to hold the ball, and my aim is horrible. My old pitching coach once told me there were twenty-seven things a pitcher has to do, all at once, in order to pitch a softball correctly. Right now, I think I'm only doing about five or six of them right, and even that may be a high estimate. As such, I throw pitch after pitch into the dirt. Our catcher, Aubree, gets beat up pretty bad trying to smother them all.

"This is going to be a long season," James says as he watches from the dugout.

"Thanks," I say. "I appreciate the vote of confidence."

I'm not really too happy with his comment, and I'm completely frustrated with my inability to throw strikes, but I do notice something different about

29

James today. For the first time, he actually puts down his phone for a few minutes and watches us practice. He definitely doesn't look impressed, not one little bit, but it's noteworthy, for it's the first time I've ever seen him show any interest in us whatsoever.

Chapter 7

Today is our first game. It's not a real game, but a scrimmage against another local team called the Mukilteo Magic. Apparently James knows the coach (I'm not certain how), so he set up the scrimmage to give us a little game experience. But it doesn't go well at all. Despite our recent practices, we are all uber rusty and we're definitely not in game shape. I'm still having a hard time throwing strikes consistently, and I walk the first four batters I face. James calls a timeout and walks out to me in the pitching circle. But once he gets there, he just stands there, looking at me, with a stupid look on his face.

"Aren't you going to say something?" I ask.

"Like what?" he asks.

"I don't know," I say. "Something coach-like. Like give me a tip, or some words of encouragement, or something to help me out."

"Throw strikes," he says.

"Thanks," I say. "That really helps. That's what I'm trying to do."

"Try harder," he says.

Without another word, he turns and walks back to the dugout.

He sits there, in the dugout, doing nothing, as I continue to struggle. I walk two more batters, then, when I finally figure out how to throw strikes, I give up two hits, then walk another batter, then give up three more hits (including a three-run homer). The Magic score six runs before we get the first out, and they score nine runs before the inning is over. It's a completely awful experience, and I'm nearly in tears as I walk slowly back to the dugout at the end of the inning.

Batting isn't any better. The Magic's pitcher is the exact opposite of me — she throws really hard, and she throws nothing but strikes. She strikes out all three of our batters (including me) in the first inning, two of three in the second, and all three in the third.

By the end of the third inning, the score is 15-0. The Magic's coach walks over and asks James if we want to continue, and mercifully he says no. We all pack up our belongings and, without a single word to one another, turn and leave.

For the first time, I start to think we made a bad decision. Maybe we should have gone to the detention center for thirty days. Even without phones, it would have been better than this.

Chapter 8

Today's practice is really somber. After being destroyed by the Mukilteo Magic in yesterday's scrimmage, none of us are happy, and we're all starting to adopt James's bad attitude. As such, we're really just going though the motions, tossing balls around the infield, really just waiting for the practice to come to an end.

But then something unexpected happens.

Judge Wilson shows up.

At first, we don't even recognize him. None of us have ever seen him without his robes on, and he walks all of the way up to the field before anyone (including James) realizes who he is. Instantly, James jumps to attention and starts barking out instructions to all of us, as though he's the coach of the year. And the rest of us pretty much do as he instructs, because we're already in a bad mood and we don't want to make things worse by getting in trouble with Judge Wilson.

Judge Wilson has a new girl with him. Her name is Emily Anderson, and apparently she's the newest addition to our team.   She's a big girl, really muscular, with dark hair and eyes. Apparently, the week before, she got caught smoking marijuana in the parking lot at her school. She joins us on the field and immediately starts working with me and the other girls. She's from a nearby town called Monroe (it's about twenty minutes east of here), and she seems a little rough around the edges, but she's nice nonetheless.

Judge Wilson watches from behind the backstop for about twenty minutes. His presence actually makes us pretty nervous, but it has one nice side effect — it makes James act like a coach (or as close to a coach as he can be) for a few minutes, and as such we actually seem like a real team for awhile. I actually have some flashbacks to our Little League days, when our coaches actually cared about us, and it reminds me of how fun those days were.

But then the most unexpected thing of all happens. James throws me a series of pitches, and I swing and miss them completely.

"Miss Parker," Judge Wilson barks. "Keep your hands up, your chin down, and watch the ball all of the way to your bat. See your bat hit the ball."

On the next three pitches, I do exactly as I was told, and the results are amazing. I hit the first pitch straight up the middle, I hit the second deep into the gap in right field, and I bounce the final off of the outfield fence. They are three of the nicest swings I have ever taken.

"That's more like it," Judge Wilson says. "Well done."

Without another word, he turns and leaves. The last thing we see is his black BMW as it exits the parking lot, turns onto Broadway, and disappears into the distance.

Chapter 9

Today is our first tournament. It's in Kent, a small city about twenty minutes east of Seattle. We have mixed emotions. We're excited, since it's the first time we've played a real game since Little League, but we're nervous, since it's our first select tournament, so we're not really certain how good the other teams are going to be. And we're still a little gun shy, too, after our disastrous scrimmage against the Mukilteo Magic.

The fields are really nice, and they are packed. There are four total, positioned around a central building which houses a concession stand and restrooms, and there are sixteen teams participating, including ours. The teams take turns playing games, and we have three total, one at 10:30 am, one at noon, and the final at 3:30 pm. We get there a little early, to warm up, and we watch a little of a 9:00 am game between two teams called the Acers and the Bobcats.

"These teams look really good," Madison says.

"You can say that again," I say as I watch the Acers' pitcher. She throws so hard the ball look likes a blur as it comes out of her hand. I wish I could throw that hard.

"That's not what I mean," Madison says

"What?" I ask.

"I mean their uniforms," she says. "Look at how sharp their uniforms are."

I have to admit she's right. The Acers are wearing black and red jerseys, with matching pants, and the Bobcats are wearing navy and white jerseys, with navy pants. They look like a million bucks.

In the meantime, we're wearing our old Little League pants and T-shirts.

"Why don't we get uniforms like that?" Kaya asks.

"Who knows," I say. "Probably because we're a bunch of misfits."

Our first game is against a team from Oregon called the Pioneers. Unfortunately, it's pretty much a replay of our scrimmage against the Magic. I struggle to throw strikes, and the entire team struggles to hit. In the meantime, the Pioneers' pitcher throws harder than any pitcher I've ever faced before, and she strikes me out twice in a row. During my final at-bat, I do a little better, and I actually manage to hit the ball, but the Pioneers' center fielder catches it easily to end the game. The final score is 12-0.

James rounds us up for a brief post-game meeting.

"Well," he says. "That was pretty much what everyone expected. We're a new team, and we're definitely going to have some growing pains. Hang in there and maybe we'll get the next one."

"Maybe?" I ask. "That doesn't sound too reassuring."

"What kind of speech was that?" Kaya asks.

"It wasn't very inspiring," Madison says.

"Give me a break," James says. "I'm new to this coaching thing. I'm still working on my post-game skills."

"Whatever," we say.

Somewhat reluctantly, we head to our next game, which is against a team from Woodinville called the Wolfpack. Their pitcher doesn't throw all that hard, and definitely not as hard as the Pioneers' pitcher, so we do a little better, but not much. The final score is 7-0. Despite the outcome, however, I actually feel somewhat good about the game, since I pitch okay (I only walk five batters, which is four fewer than our last game). In addition, I remember to do what Judge Wilson told me when I'm batting (hands up, chin down, eyes on the ball), and I get my first hit, a nice single straight up the middle.

After our game, we have a small break, and James takes us to lunch at Subway, which is surprisingly pretty fun. We goof around a little, and even James seems like he's in a pretty good mood, which is strange since he's never enjoyed being our coach (most of us are surprised he offered to take us anywhere). He even jokes around a little, and he compliments my hit.

"I knew it was a single the minute you hit it," he says. "That shortstop never had a chance."

A funny thing happens a few minutes later. He gets up to go to the restroom, but he accidentally leaves his phone sitting on the table. I reach over to grab it, so I can give it back to him when he returns, when I see something interesting on its screen. There is an icon for something called *Softball Skills*. I look at it more closely and see it's some sort of 'How To' e-book for softball coaches. I click on it and see it's half read.

None of us can believe it.

"James is reading an e-book about softball?" Kaya asks.

"Why?" Madison asks. "I thought he hates softball."

"Who knows?" I say. "Maybe he's finally coming around. Maybe he'll turn into a good coach yet."

We'd all like to see that happen, but we're not getting our hopes up.

Not yet.

Our third and final game of the day is against a team from Redmond called the Mustangs. We get off to a good start, and we actually take the lead for awhile. Kaya hits a double, and Madison drives her in with a single to left. I follow Madison's single with a double to right, and Madison scores all of the way from first. We hold the lead until the third, when three consecutive Mustang batters get hits off of me. The game remains tied 2-2 until the fifth, when Kaya hits another double and scores when I follow with a single. Unfortunately, the Mustangs come back and get three runs in the sixth, and they end up winning 5-3. We're all disappointed we lost, but at the same time, it was a pretty good game. James's post-game speech is pretty much as weak as ever, but overall we don't care, and we actually feel pretty good about ourselves. We lost all three games, but we clearly made some progress.

As we head for our cars in the parking lot, I spot someone noteworthy leaving the stands.

Judge Wilson.

Chapter 10

Today we have our first review hearing. Apparently, according to James, a review hearing is something that is routinely done in cases like ours, to make certain defendants in criminal cases (in other words, us) are doing what we're supposed to be doing and complying with the judge's orders. Like always, we sit at the defense table, with James at our side. He is wearing a fancy navy suit with gray pinstripes, and it's actually kinda strange to me now. For the past six weeks, I've seen him at our practices, usually in sweat pants or blue jeans, and I've kinda forgotten what he looks like when he's all fancied up.

Unlike our last hearing, which was just the four of us (me, Madison, Kaya, and Jennie), Aubree and Emily are here, too. Apparently, since we're all on the Missfits, Judge Wilson decided to consolidate our hearings.

"It's called judicial economy," James explains.

The clerk at the front of the room stands up and faces us. "Everyone rise," he says. "This court will now come to session. The Honorable Judge Thomas H. Wilson III, presiding."

We all stand up as Judge Wilson, wearing his long, flowing, black robes, enters the room and takes his place on the judge's stand above us.

"Good afternoon," he says.

"Good afternoon," we all say.

"Today is our first review hearing," he says. "I've reviewed the file, and the progress report submitted by Mr. Kingsley, and I'm pretty happy. It appears you ladies are in compliance with my sentence. All practices have been completed, as ordered, and you even competed in your first tournament. Not bad. And you've all stayed out of trouble in the meantime. Do you ladies have anything to say?"

We all look at each other, but we're all silent.

"What do you think so far?" he asks. "Do you think my idea was crazy, or is it turning out okay? Do you like softball? Miss Parker, you usually have something to say. What do you think?"

"It's okay," I say. "We made a little progress this weekend. The first game was brutal, but the final game was fun. I actually thought we were going to win for awhile."

"I thought so, too," Judge Wilson says. "I was impressed. There is still plenty of room for improvement, there's no doubt about that, but overall you played a good game, and you're definitely on the right track. Miss Miller, that was a nice catch you made in the third inning. Way to hustle to that ball. Miss Suzuki, that was some nice batting you did. Two hits a day will make any coach happy. Miss Johnson, excellent defense. Same for you, Miss Tanner, and you, Miss Anderson. Nothing gets by the three of you. And Miss Parker, the pitching is coming along nicely, as is your batting. Always remember to keep your hands up."

"Yes, sir," I say.

"But," Judge Wilson says, "there is one thing I wasn't happy about. Not at all."

We all get nervous. For a brief second, the room is as silent as a library.

Judge Wilson turns to James. "Mr. Kingsley," he says. "Why were the ladies wearing T-shirts at the tournament? The Missfits are a select team. Select teams do not wear T-shirts."

James's eyes grow large, and he instantly rises to answer the question.

"Sir," he says. "With all due respect, your honor was most gracious in allotting us $1,000 from the court's registry, but to be honest, $1,000 doesn't go very far these days. We needed some bats, and they are $300 a piece, for good ones. In addition, none of the ladies had mouth guards, or sliding pads, or batting gloves."

"I had a pair from Little League," I say, "but they were missing two fingers."

"So," James continues, "I felt I had no choice but to spend the money on necessities. Especially safety items, like mouth guards. To me, fancy uniforms are a luxury."

Judge Wilson nods. "I see," he says. "I understand, but I'm not certain I agree. In my experience, young ladies like to look good when they play, so I think nice uniforms are a necessity. What do you think? Miss Parker, would you like nice uniforms?"

"It would be nice," I say.

"I agree," Judge Wilson says. He turns to his law clerk, who is a young man named Hugh Webber. "Mr. Webber, please hand the ladies their new uniforms."

Hugh pulls a large box from under a nearby table and carries it over to us. We open it and pull out some of the nicest softball uniforms I have ever seen.

41

They are navy and gold, with white stripes down the sides. The word 'Missfits' is printed on the front, in fancy lettering, and our names and numbers are on the back. I'm #24. They have matching pants with fancy stripes.

"Well," Judge Wilson says. "What do you think?"

"They're awesome," I say.

"I thought you'd like them," he says. "I'm not very good with fashion, so I had my granddaughter help me design them. She's good with that type of thing." He turns to James. "Mr. Kinglsey, there's some stuff in there for you, too. A team's coach needs to look good, too."

We dig through the box, and sure enough, there is a jacket and baseball cap for James. Both match our uniforms perfectly.

"Thank you, your honor," James says. He looks as surprised as the rest of us. Even he doesn't know what to say.

Judge Wilson holds up a cap. "I got one for myself, too," he says. "Go Missfits."

Chapter 11

Today is our second tournament. Everyone is excited, since we're hoping to continue our improvement and build off of the success we had at our first tournament. But the thing that excites us the most is the fact we get to wear our new uniforms for the first time. I don't mean to sound conceited or anything, but we look good. I see players from other teams shoot us glances as they see us for the first time.

The tournament is at a community college in Mount Vernon, a small city about an hour north of Seattle. There are two fields, with games on each field, and ten teams participating. The weather is really nice, and it promises to be a fun day if we play well.

And we do. Our first game is against a team from Seattle called the Spice. They're a good team, but not overly so, and we stay with them for most of the game. They finally win it in the top of the seventh, but no one is too upset, since the score ends up being 8-7, which is the closest game we've had so far.

"Not bad, ladies," James says. He's wearing his new jacket and cap, and with them on, he actually looks like a softball coach. "Not bad at all. At the rate we're progressing, some wins are right around the corner."

He's not mistaken. Our next game is against a team from Spokane called the Skyhawks, and it's a really good game. For the first time ever, I don't walk a single batter, and I strike out six, which is a personal best (my previous high was four, against the Spice). Almost every girl on our team gets a hit, and Kaya wins it for us by hitting a double that scores Madison all of the way from second. The final score is 5-4, and we celebrate heartily. If I didn't know better, I'd think we just won the World Series. Even James, who never wanted to be a coach in the first place, is all smiles afterward, and he goes around clapping everyone on the back and telling them how well they played.

Unfortunately, our glory is short lived. Our next game, and our final of the day, is against a team called the Bellevue Beast. They are amazing. Their pitcher is a girl named Sydney Jameson, and she throws crazy hard, and she strikes me out easily every time I face her. None of my teammates do any better, and Emily gets our only hit, a bloop single in the fourth. In the meantime, the Beast batters tear me up, and I give up nine runs, five off of home runs. During one inning, in the midst of their hit parade, James has to call a timeout and come out to the pitching circle to calm me down.

"It's okay," he says. "This is a really good team. By far the best we've ever faced. We're not quite at their level yet. Just do your best, and we'll be fine."

His advice doesn't help my performance any, but it does settle me down a lot, and we move on from there. The final score is 9-0. Amazingly, however, the crushing loss doesn't dampen our spirits too much, since we're all happy we got our first win. At our level, and at this point in time, one win a day will suffice.

But something interesting happens at the end of the game. As I'm rounding up my belongings and placing them back in my softball bag, I hear the Beast coach, who is standing a few feet to the side, talking to one of his players. I immediately recognize her, since she's a really good player, and she hit two home runs off of me during the game. The second was a monster shot to left center. I knew it was gone the minute she hit it. But I ended up getting a little redemption in the end, since I struck her out during her last at-bat (she was the only girl I struck out the whole game).

"What have I told you about changeups?" the coach asks. His face is red, and he's clearly angry.

"I've got to wait longer," the girl says, "before swinging. I've got to be patient."

"Exactly," the coach says. "So why didn't you?"

"It's hard," she says. "I get so impatient, I just can't wait. I'm still trying to figure it out."

"Well you better figure it out soon," he says. "Because I'm getting tired of sitting around watching you strike out all day."

"I only struck out once," she says.

"And once the game before that," the coach says. "And once the game before that. Always on changeups. Day after day we work on changeups, and day after day you screw them up. I'm getting sick of it."

"I got two home runs," she says. "And I got two last week. That's pretty good, right?"

"Not good enough," the coach says. "You're a good player, Payton, but good isn't enough. This is the Beast. We're an elite team, and if you want to stay on an elite team, you better learn how to hit a changeup. Otherwise, I'm going to cut you. I'm sick of wasting my time."

Without another word, he turns and stomps away.

I can hardly believe what I just saw. I may be new to the world of select softball, but I never expected it to be like this. In my mind, a girl who hit two home runs in one game should be walking away as the hero, with a big smile on her face.

Not this girl. This girl, Payton, walks away with tears running down her cheeks.

Chapter 12

Today's practice starts off pretty normal, with a couple of warm-up laps, some stretching, and some catch. After that, James, who has apparently finished reading his e-book about softball coaching, rounds us up and leads us through some drills he learned in his book. The drills are all pretty routine, and I remember doing some of them back in Little League, but still it's kind of nice seeing him finally take a little interest in coaching.

The highlight of practice, however, comes about twenty minutes later. I'm standing on one side of the field, with our catcher, working on my pitching (my curveball is getting a little better every day) as James runs through a series of throwing drills with most of the other girls on the far side of the field. I take a small break and grab my water bottle out of the dugout when a girl walks up. She's dressed in a sweatshirt and sweatpants and has a softball bag over one shoulder. At first I don't recognize her, but when she removes her hoodie and shakes her hair free, I remember exactly who she is.

It's Payton, the really good center fielder who plays for the Beast. The same player who got yelled at by her coach and left the field in tears after our last game.

"Hi," she says.

"Hi," I say.

"I was wondering," she said. "If you guys have any spots open on your team. I'd like to join if you have a spot available."

I can hardly believe what I just heard.

"You want to join our team?" I ask.

"Yeah," she says. "I quit the Beast. I can't take Mr. Moran any more. He yells at me every day. I do my best, honestly I do, but it's never good enough."

My eyes get big. I can hardly believe what is happening. A player as good as Payton wants to play for us? Adding her to our team would make us twice as good as before.

Tempting as it is, however, I have to be honest with her.

"We're a new team," I say. "We're not very good. We've only won one game so far. Most of the others were blowouts. Just like the game against your team."

"I don't care about that," she says. "I just want to have some fun. On the Beast, there is no such thing as fun. It's all about winning. That's all Mr. Moran cares about. I like your coach better."

I shoot a glance at James on the far side of the field. Almost on cue, a stray ball flies across the field and hits him on the shoulder.

"Our coach has some issues, too," I say.

Payton shrugs. "They all do," she says. "But I saw how he reacted during our game. Even though you were struggling, and you gave up all of those home runs, he told you it was no big deal. Mr. Moran would have gone crazy if our pitcher gave up that many home runs."

My eyes get big. To be honest, I'm a little offended.

48

Payton sees my reaction and instantly tries to clarify her statement. "I'm sorry," she says. "I didn't mean to say you were doing poorly. I know you were doing your best. It's just that on the Beast doing your best isn't good enough."

I'm not certain her explanation is all that great, but I understand what she means, and I smile. "It's okay," I say. "I can check with James and see if you can join. Since he's the coach he's in charge. But I think he'll be fine with it. I don't see why not. We could always use another player. Especially someone as good as you."

"Thanks," Payton says. "I'll be honest, though. I can't hit a changeup to save my life. Fastballs, curveballs, screws — I can hit all of those, easily, but not changeups. But tell him I'll give 100% effort, and I'll work as hard as he wants. I never dog it."

"Okay," I say. "I'll be right back."

I walk over and get James. I tell him about Payton, and he instantly comes over to meet her. He seems as surprised as I am.

"I'm James," he says, shaking her hand. "It's nice to meet you, Payton."

"It's nice to meet you, Mr.—"

She pauses, since she doesn't know James's last name.

"You can call me James," he says.

Her eyes get big. "Really?" she asks. "Mr. Moran would freak if we called him by his first name. To be honest, I don't even know what his first name is."

"Well," James says, "I'm not Mr. Moran."

"Sweet," Payton says. "Anyway, James, if you'll let me join the team, I promise I'll do my best, and I never miss practices, and I can play any position except pitcher and catcher."

"Sounds good to me," James says.

"And I'll do a tryout if you want," Payton continues. "And I can get references from some of my former coaches if you want. Not Mr. Moran, of course, but coaches from my teams before the Beast."

James smiles. "I don't think that'll be necessary, Payton," he says. "If you want to join the team, you're welcome. You're actually more than welcome. Put your stuff in the dugout and I'll introduce you to everyone else."

I can't believe it. Just like that, we've added a new player. And a good one. With her, we might actually become a good team after all. Maybe even a great one.

Chapter 13

Practice is really fun with Payton on the team. She's amazing, both hitting and fielding. She says she's played softball as long as she remembers, so she knows more than anyone else, and as such she becomes James's informal assistant. She gives us tips and advice, and she helps James run many of our exercises and drills. In no time, our spirits are flying high and our improvement, at the risk of sounding arrogant, is meteoric. The only bad thing about Payton, however, is the fact she has one glaring weakness. For some inexplicable reason, and no matter how hard she tries, she cannot hit changeups.

"What's up with that?" I ask.

She shrugs. "I've never been able to hit changeups," she says. "I just don't have the patience. They take so long to get to the plate. I just can't wait long enough. So I miss them every time."

We try to help her, and even James tries to give her some advice, but nothing works. Every time I throw her a changeup, she flails at it fruitlessly. To be honest, sometimes it's so bad it's embarrassing.

"Thank goodness," Payton says, "few people know my weakness. Otherwise, they could throw me nothing but changeups, and I'd strike out every time."

Chapter 14

Our tournament today is in Redmond, a city about ten minutes east of Seattle, just past Lake Washington. The weather isn't great, and the sky is dark and gray, which is pretty typical in the Pacific Northwest, but it doesn't dampen our enthusiasm at all. We can't wait to get on the field with our new star player (Payton) and see how we do.

But then things get even better. As we're warming up for our first game, Judge Wilson walks up. He's wearing his Missfits hat, and he's got a big smile on his face. James jogs over to greet him.

"How are we looking today, Coach?" Judge Wilson asks.

"Good," James says. "The girls are pretty excited. We got a new player this week, a girl who used to play for the Beast, and she's making her debut."

"Excellent," Judge Wilson says. "Speaking of new players, I brought you one more. This is my granddaughter, Kaitlin."

Standing at Judge Wilson's side, with a softball bag over her shoulder, is a tall, thin girl, approximately fifteen, with long, dark hair and brown eyes.

"Excuse me?" James asks.

"Kaitlin normally plays for the Washington Wildcats," Judge Wilson explains, "but her team has the weekend off. So I thought it would be fun if she played pick-up with you this weekend, if that's okay."

My eyes get big the minute I hear the name Washington Wildcats. Being new to the select softball world, I still don't know a whole lot, but I've overheard other girls talking about the Wildcats, and their story is always the same — the Wildcats are one of the best teams in the state. All of their players are excellent.

Kaitlin is no exception. She slips into a spare Missfits uniform, then joins us on the field, and we are immediately impressed. She's as good as Payton, maybe better. She throws the ball so hard it sounds like an explosion when it hits my mitt. When she takes grounders in the infield, nothing gets past her. And when she does her warm-up swings, every hit is straight up the middle. It's like watching a batting machine in action.

So now we're totally jazzed. We have not one, but two great players to add to our squad. Granted, Kaitlin is only a pick-up player, so she's probably only going to play with us for the weekend, but we're grateful anyway, and we'll take whatever help we can get.

Our first game is against a team from Wenatchee called the Wings. They're good, and their pitcher is a heavy, blond girl who throws a bunch of nasty pitches, but she's no match for us, especially for Payton and Kaitlin. Payton hits two doubles and a triple, Kaitlin gets three doubles, and the rest of us chip in as needed. I get two singles, one of which scores three runs (I love batting when the bases are loaded). In the meantime, my pitching is solid (definitely the best I've done so far), and I only walk two batters the entire game. In the meantime, I strike out five, and we cruise to an easy win, 6-0.

"Well done, ladies," Judge Wilson calls from the stands. "Well done indeed."

Our dugout is nothing but smiles as we round up our stuff and head for our next game, which is on an adjacent field. We can hardly believe it, but in a span of two months, we have turned into a pretty solid team. We all know we're not championship caliber yet, but we're on our way.

Our next game is as fun as the first. Much to my delight, Kaitlin can pitch, too (for all I know, she can do everything). So James has her pitch, and he has me play shortstop, which is my secondary position. This is a real treat for me, because it gives me a break from pitching and takes a little pressure off of me (it's pretty tough when you have to pitch multiple games in a row). Our game is against a team from British Columbia called the Bombers. Like most Canadian teams, they're really good, and they're really big. Most of the girls look like they're in their late teens, but I know that can't be true since this is a tournament for girls under sixteen. Regardless, Kaitlin is not intimidated in the least. She comes out throwing nothing but strikes, and she doesn't give up a single hit until the bottom of the fourth inning. In the meantime, we come out with our bats red hot, and I get things started with a nice single to left center. Kaitlin lays down a perfect sacrifice bunt that moves me to second, and Payton hits a shot off of the outfield wall to score me easily. Kaya follows with a single, scoring Payton, and Madison drives her in with a line-drive to left field.

Before we know it, we're ahead 4-0.

The final score is 7-1. The Bombers' only run comes in the bottom of the sixth, when the Bombers' first baseman, who is a tall girl with long, red hair, hits a solo home run to center.

"I can't believe I'm about to say this," Jennie says. "But we're on a winning streak."

"I never thought I'd see the day," I say.

"Me, neither," James says. "But let's make the most of it."

Our third (and final) game of the day is on another field, so we move over to it and start to unpack our gear. It's against a team from Seattle called Seattle Fastpitch. I take over the pitching duties again, but this game turns out to be much more difficult than the first two. I struggle a little in the first inning, and I have a tough time throwing strikes consistently. The Seattle Fastpitch players take advantage of my woes, and by the time the inning is over, we're losing 2-0.

"That's okay," James says. "We can get those runs back. Hang in there, ladies."

It turns out he is right. Payton and Kaitlin lead the way with their bats, and by the third inning, the score is tied 3-3. By this time I've settled down and I'm pitching quite well, but I've got to be really careful, because I can tell how good these batters are, and I know if I make any mistakes, they'll take advantage and clobber me.

It turns out to be a back-and-forth, hard fought, well-played game. Seattle Fastpitch takes the lead in the fourth, 4-3, when their catcher nails one of my fastballs to straightaway center, but Payton answers with a home run of her own to tie it at 4-4. Kaitlin hits a home run in the sixth to give us the lead momentarily, but unfortunately I just can't hold onto it for long, and we end up losing in the bottom of the seventh when I give up back-to-back doubles. The final score is 6-5.

I'm pretty heartbroken, since we were doing so well, and at first I feel like I let the whole team down, but my agony is short-lived. Judge Wilson walks into the dugout with a big smile on his face.

"Well done ladies," he says. "That was a fun game."

"We lost," I say.

He shrugs. "You can't win them all," he says. "But boy was it exciting." He turns to Kaitlin. "It reminded me of that game you had last year against the Eastside Angels. The one that went into extra innings."

"That was a fun game," Kaitlin says. "I was sweating bullets the whole time."

Judge Wilson laughs. "I can't wait 'til tomorrow," he says. "More action awaits. Go Missfits."

The next day, we're back on the field. We're excited because this is our first two-day tournament, and we want to see if we can start a new winning streak. In addition, this tournament is one of the ones that crowns a champion, so if we can play well and win some games, we might be able to walk away with a shiny trophy.

But the pressure is intense, since it's single elimination. You get to keep playing until you lose a game. Once you lose, your day is over.

Our first game is against a team we've already played, back in our first tournament, called the Woodinville Wolfpack. They beat us 7-0 in that first tournament, but we were a different team back then, so we're not intimidated. Kaitlin pitches and, just like the day before, she is awesome. She throws nothing but strikes. The Wolfpack get a couple of runs, but they never really threaten to do much serious damage. In the meantime, Emily gets two doubles, Payton launches a massive home run to left, and we win 5-2. I finish the game 1-3 with a single and a walk.

Our next game is against a team called the Bobcats. I've seen them before, but we've never played them, so we don't really know much about them. They're a small team, but they're lightning fast, and they like to play 'small ball.' Their batters are primarily bunters and slappers, so we're forced to play really solid defense, which we do. Payton gets another home run, Kaitlin adds a triple and a double, and Madison gets two singles. We win 4-1.

Now we're getting really excited. We've won two games in a row, and if we win the next one, we'll be in the championship game. And if we win that game, the trophy is ours.

Unfortunately, it isn't meant to be. Our next game is against a team from Tacoma called the Tide, and they're awesome. Their pitcher is a tall, heavy girl with dark hair and mean eyes. She looks like the type of girl who beats up kittens for the fun of it. She throws the ball crazy hard. Kaitlin and Payton do okay against her (Kaitlin gets a double and Payton gets two singles), but the rest of us are hopeless. I strike out all three times. We lose, and the final score is 3-0.

Amazingly, and somewhat to my surprise, I'm not too disappointed. I wanted to win the game, and get a shiny trophy, but to be honest, I'm still pretty happy. Total, we won four of six games this weekend.

That's not bad, for a bunch of Missfits.

Chapter 15

Our next tournament is in Federal Way, a city about thirty minutes south of Seattle. It rains off-and-on all day, but never enough to cancel or postpone any of our games. Like the week before, Kaitlin's team isn't playing, so she plays with us again. That gets us all excited, since she's a great player, and she's also a nice girl. We even take some time before the first game to learn a little about her.

"What's it like being a judge's granddaughter?" I ask.

Kaitlin shrugs. "It's no big deal," she says. "He gets kinda high-and-mighty on occasion, but I just tell him to get over it, and he does. And, like most grandfathers, he spoils me rotten, so I don't complain."

"At first," Madison says, "he seemed so grumpy in the courtroom. But now he seems different. Especially when he's here watching softball."

Kaitlin nods. "He loves softball," she says. "I think he likes it even more than I do. He's been going to my games ever since I was in Little League. I don't think he's missed a game since. He even postponed one of his trials once so it wouldn't interfere with my game. And he flies down to see my sister in LA whenever he can."

"You have a sister in LA?" I ask.

Kaitlin nods. "Her name is Alyssa. She's a sophomore at UCLA. She plays for UCLA's softball team."

We're in complete awe. We all looked up to Kaitlin before, but now she's at goddess level. An older sister at UCLA? How cool is that?

"My grandfather was a little disappointed at first," she says, "because he went to the University of Washington, so he wanted Alyssa to play there, but when UCLA offered her a scholarship, he got over it pretty quickly. And I love having her at UCLA, 'cause traveling to California is always fun. And I got her bedroom when she moved out, so that was cool, too."

We all laugh. Unfortunately, we don't get to discuss things any further. Our first game is about to begin, and we take the field. It's against a team from Oregon called the Blazers. They're noteworthy because they wear the ugliest uniforms I have ever seen. They're neon yellow, with orange and red letters that are shaped like flames. They're so bright I have to wear my sunglasses so I can look at them. The Blazers themselves, however, are pretty good, but we manage to take a quick lead, then hang on to win 3-1. I get a double, Payton gets a triple, and Kaitlin adds two singles.

Our second and third games are more of the same. Our second game is against a team from our last tournament, the Wenatchee Wings. Unlike the Blazers, the Wings wear normal, blue and white uniforms, so I'm actually able to take my sunglasses off. Kaitlin pitches and is excellent. She overwhelms the Wings' batters, and they only get three hits the whole game. In the meantime, their pitcher struggles, and we beat her up something fierce. I get a double,

Jennie gets a triple, and Kaitlin and Payton add solo home runs. The final score is 6-0.

Our third game is against a team called the Acers, and we win 4-3. We all clap each other on the backs, and several players exchange hugs. We're really happy, because it's the first time we've won three games in a row, and the first time we've won all three games in a day. This tournament is another two-day event, so we can't wait for the following day, and another chance at a shiny trophy.

The next day, something unexpected (and really bad) happens. Our first game is against Payton's old team, the Bellevue Beast.

The minute we learn who our opponent is, Payton transforms. She becomes a completely different person than normal. Since joining us, she has been happy, carefree, and nothing but fun. To be honest, she's the perfect teammate. But now, she's totally different. She's quiet, and withdrawn, and clearly nervous. She stares across the field at the opposing dugout and glares at the Beast's coach, Mr. Moran.

"I hate him," she says. "I want to beat him so bad."

So we make it a team goal. We're all grateful to Payton, for all she's done to help us so far, so we want to give her something in return. We're going to play our hearts out, if that's what it takes, to win this game for Payton.

Unfortunately, beating the Beast is easier said than done. They are undoubtedly the best team I've ever seen, and they're even better than the Tacoma Tide. They may be as good as the Washington Wildcats.

"We've got to be patient," Payton says. "Their pitcher is a girl named Sydney Jameson. She throws really hard, but she tends to get tired, especially late in games. So that's when she's most vulnerable."

"The other thing we've got to do," Kaitlin says, "is watch for her curveball. She can't control it as well as her other pitches, so she tends to leave it over the plate on occasion. If she does, hammer it."

We all shoot glances at her. We understand Payton's knowledge of the Beast, since she used to play for them, but how does Kaitlin know the things she knows?

"I've played the Beast many times," she says, "over the years. My team, the Wildcats, and the Beast are arch rivals. We've met in more championship games than I can remember. Payton will recall the last."

"The Beast won," Payton says.

"Only because you played dirty," Kaitlin says. "Your pitcher was throwing at our heads. On purpose."

We all look at Payton, and we're incredulous. We can't believe what we just heard.

"Is it true?" I ask.

Payton hesitates briefly, then nods. "Sydney didn't want to do it, and the rest of us didn't like it either, but she had no choice. Mr. Moran told her if she didn't do it he would kick her off of the team. And we knew he was serious 'cause he's kicked girls off of the team before."

"Why would he do that?" I ask. "It's against the rules to throw a pitch at someone's head. And it's so dangerous."

"I already told you," Payton says. "Mr. Moran doesn't care about the rules. Or about safety. All he cares about is winning. That's why I quit the team."

We all shrug. Now we're not so certain. We want to win, for Payton, but I'll be honest — we're afraid. The Beast's pitcher, Sydney, throws hard. We don't want her to throw pitches at our heads.

Luckily, she doesn't, at least at the beginning of the game. Kaitlin pitches for us, and it's a classic pitcher's duel. Both girls are awesome, and neither team gets a run through the first five innings. But then, as predicted, Sydney starts to get tired, and we make a breakthrough. Kaitlin hits a double, and Kaya follows it with a single to left, which scores Kaitlin from second (the throw to home is close, but Kaitlin is extremely fast and slides under the catcher's tag).

So we lead 1-0, with only two innings to go. I glance over at Payton, who is playing center, and there is hope in her eyes. She's only six outs away from beating her old team and her personal nemesis, Mr. Moran.

Speaking of Mr. Moran, he is irate. He paces around his dugout, and at one point, he kicks over a water cooler. He can't believe his 'elite' team is losing to the Missfits.

Unfortunately, we're unable to hold the lead. As I've said before, Kaitlin is a great pitcher, but the Beast batters are good, too, and finally they find a chink in her armor. Their second baseman hits a single to left, and their center fielder follows it with a massive home run to straightaway.

They lead 2-1.

Luckily, we get out of the inning without any more damage (Kaitlin recovers and strikes out the next two batters), and the score remains 2-1 until the bottom of the seventh.

At this point, as you can probably imagine, the tension is palpable. We all want to win for Payton, but our backs are against the wall. This is the final inning, so it's now or never.

We put up quite a fight. The Beast pitcher, Sydney, gets the first two outs, but then I keep things alive by hitting a single to right. Kaitlin follows with another single, and I advance to third. I slide into the base just under the third baseman's tag.

So that's where we sit. Losing by one, with two outs in the bottom of the final inning, with runners on first and third. If our next batter gets out, the game is over, and we lose. But if she gets a hit, I'll score for sure, and if she gets a big hit (a double or better), Kaitlin will score as well.

That would give us the win.

Guess who our next batter is.

Of all people, it's Payton.

Payton, the former Beast, is going to face her old team with the entire game on the line. She walks up to the plate, a look of sheer determination in her eyes. She takes a deep breath, and I can tell she's nervous. Big time.

Mr. Moran sees who's up, calls a timeout, and rushes to the pitching circle to talk to Sydney. Like always, they turn their backs to us, so we can't hear their conversation, but from my place on third base, I can hear tidbits anyway.

"Mr. Moran," Sydney says. "That isn't fair."

"Who cares," Mr. Moran says. "Do it anyway."

"But —"

"Do it," Mr. Moran says. "Or else. Do you understand me?"

There is a long silence.

"Do you understand me?" Mr. Moran says.

"Yes, sir," Sydney says. She does not sound happy. Not in the least.

Mr. Moran walks slowly back to the dugout. There is a wry smile on his lips.

I stand there in complete shock. To be perfectly honest, I'm terrified out of my mind. I'm absolutely certain he just told Sydney to throw the pitch at Payton's head. I want to do something, to stop it from happening, but I don't know what to do. Should I call a timeout, so I can tell James? Maybe he could do something. At a minimum he could warn Payton, or he could file an objection with the umpire.

I never get a chance to do anything. As I stand there, trying to decide what to do, Sydney makes the pitch.

For once in my life, I'm ecstatic I'm wrong. The pitch doesn't go anywhere near Payton's head.

But for Payton, it's equally devastating. It's a changeup, and a nasty one at that. It's at least fifteen miles per hour slower than Sydney's normal pitches.

Payton swings and misses by a mile.

The catcher throws the ball back to Sydney. Sydney looks over at Mr. Moran.

"Again," he says.

The second pitch is another changeup. This one is even slower than the first.

Payton misses it by a mile.

"Again," Mr. Moran says.

Sydney takes a deep breath, and she clearly doesn't want to do it, but she has no choice.

One pitch later, the game is over.

And so is the tournament.

And so is our chance at a shiny trophy.

And so is Payton's chance to get even with Mr. Moran.

Payton is so embarrassed and frustrated she throws her bat down and collapses in a heap in the dugout, crying her eyes out. We all run over, and we try to comfort her and help her feel better, but she's nearly hysterical she's so upset. James sees what has happened and he storms onto the field, his face red, and he challenges Mr. Moran.

"What was that?" he asks.

"What do you mean?" Mr. Moran asks. "It was a good game, Coach. You came up a little short. Better luck next time."

"It was not a good game," James says. He's really angry now. "You played dirty. You knew she had a weakness and you exploited it."

"So?" Mr. Moran says. "That's how you win, right? Find the other team's weakness and take advantage of it?"

"These are girls," James says. His voice is really loud, and he's nearly shouting now. He and Mr. Moran are really close, their faces just inches apart. "These aren't professional athletes. You don't treat them like that."

"I do what I want," Mr. Moran says.

"Not when I'm around," James says.

"What are you going to do?" Mr. Moran says.

For a brief, terrifying second, I actually think James is going to punch him in the face. But at the last second, he steadies himself, calms down, and turns to leave.

"Your time will come," he says. "I guarantee it. And we'll be there when you fall."

At that, he returns to our dugout. Several of our parents, and Judge Wilson, are in the dugout now, and with their help we've finally been able to calm Payton down a little. We all take turns giving her hugs, and she leaves with her dad.

James rounds the rest of us up for our traditional post-game discussion. He, too, has calmed down, but I can tell he's still pretty upset, and to be honest I've never seen him like this before.

"All in all," he says, "it was a good weekend. You all did well. Kaitlin, thanks again for playing with us, and you're always welcome to join us in the future. Starting tomorrow, however, we're going to double our practices. We're going to start working twice as hard as normal, and we're going to become the best team in the state, and we're going to beat that son of a _____."

I'll let you fill in the final word, but let's just say it starts with the letter b, and it rhymes with the word witch.

"Is that okay with you?" he asks.

"Yes, sir," we say, in unison. Nothing would make us happier than beating the Beast.

"For Payton," he says.

"For Payton," we say.

At that, our mission officially begins. If it's the last thing we do, we are going to beat the Beast. And when I say the Beast, I don't mean the team.

I mean Mr. Moran.

Chapter 16

Apparently, when James decides to get serious about something, he doesn't fool around. He walks up to today's practice with two men at his sides. The first man, on his right, is tall and lean, with a thick, black goatee and matching hair. The other man is shorter, with intense eyes and short, cropped, graying hair.

"Ladies," James says. "I'd like to introduce you to Steven Smith and Donnie Douglas. Steven and Donnie are assistant coaches for Western Washington University, up in Bellingham, and they're going to be working with us for the next month or so. Steven is Western's batting coach, so he's going to be helping us with our hitting. Donnie is Western's pitching coach, so he's going to be working with Paige and our catchers. Without further adieu, let's get to it."

We break into two groups, with the majority of the girls following Steven and James to the batting cages on the far side of the field. I stay with Donnie and the catchers, and he leads us to the bullpen to work on my pitching.

"Let's see a couple of pitches," he says. "Start with fastballs."

I do as told.

"Not bad," he says. "Now let me see a curve."

I throw a curve.

"Now a changeup."

I throw a changeup.

"Not bad," he says. "You've definitely got potential. You've got your basics down, and physically you're ideal. Long legs, long arms, not bad. But to be honest, none of that means a thing to me. Do you know why?"

I raise an eyebrow. "Why?" I ask.

"Great pitchers don't have to have long arms and long legs," he says, "to be good. It helps, but it isn't necessary. But there is one thing you've got to have. Without it, you'll never be great. Do you know what it is?"

"Not really," I say.

"Desire," he says. "You've got to have a burning desire to succeed. A desire to always want to improve. A desire to do whatever it takes, no matter how much work is involved. Do you have that desire, Paige?"

"I guess so," I say.

"Then let's see it," he says. "Drop and give me fifty push-ups."

"Fifty?" I ask.

I can hardly believe it. The most I've ever done before is thirty. Fifty will probably kill me. My arms might fall off.

"Fifty," he says.

Not knowing what else to do, I toss my mitt to the side, drop to the ground, and start doing push-ups. It isn't easy, and I have to stop and take a break (twice), but somehow I struggle through.

"Well done," he says. "Now do fifty crunches."

I'm still breathing heavily from the push-ups, but I do as told, and somehow I struggle through fifty crunches. My abs are burning by the time I'm done.

"Excellent," he says. "That's true desire. We may be able to make a star out of you yet." But then he turns to our catchers, Aubree and Hannah, who have been standing next to him, watching me do my exercises.

"What are you doing?" he asks. "What kind of catcher stands around, watching, as her pitcher does all of the work? Give me fifty."

"Push-ups or crunches?" Aubree asks.

"Both," he says.

Neither girl looks happy, but they do as told. By the time they're done, they're breathing heavily and covered in sweat (just like me). To be honest, we look like a mess.

As soon as they finish, Donnie turns back to me. "You've had plenty of time to rest," he says. "Give me fifty more."

"Really?" I ask. I can hardly believe what I just heard.

"You want to be a star, don't you?" he asks. "James tells me you want to beat the Beast. You think that's going to be easy? They're probably practicing right now. And I bet their pitcher can do push-ups and crunches in her sleep."

I sigh, then drop to the ground and do another set of push-ups. Somewhere around thirty, my arms start to lock up, and for a few brief seconds I think they might actually break off at the elbows. But somehow I push on, and amazingly I'm able to finish.

But then Donnie turns back to the catchers.

"Oh my goodness," he says. "Are you two standing around again? What kind of catchers stand around when their pitcher is suffering? Give me fifty."

This becomes the routine for the rest of practice. Push-ups, crunches, more push-ups, more crunches. At one point, we actually start working on some pitching, but we never get to do much before we get to do another set of push-ups and crunches. After awhile I can barely lift my arms above my shoulders they are so tired.

"What's going on?" Donnie asks. He's not happy with my most recent pitch. "Your velocity has dropped significantly. Your earlier pitches were much harder than that."

"I'm tired," I say. "And I can barely feel my arms."

"That's no excuse," Donnie says. "Much of your velocity comes from your snap. So focus on your snap, and if you do it correctly, your velocity will stay sharp even when you're tired."

I sigh, but not knowing what else to do, I follow his instructions. On my next pitch, I put all of my concentration into my wrist, and I snap it as hard as I can just as I release the ball. It sounds like a small explosion as it hits the catcher's mitt.

"See," he says. "That was excellent. That pitch was at least five miles per hour faster than the last one. Maybe more. Try it again. Focus on nothing but your snap."

My next pitch is even faster than the last.

And the one after that is even faster than it.

My eyes get big, and my heart races. I've never been able to throw that hard before, not consistently, even when I'm fully rested. Donnie really knows what he's talking about. In one practice, he's already taught me something extremely important.

Unfortunately, my excitement is short-lived. Five minutes later, I'm back on the ground, doing push-ups and crunches again.

Chapter 17

Today's practice is much like yesterday's. Donnie works me and the catchers like we're dogs, but I'm willing to do whatever he says, no matter how painful it is, because I'm convinced he knows what he's doing. He has me focus completely on my snaps, and he pulls out a radar gun and checks the speed of my pitches. The first few are around fifty miles an hour. An hour later, my pitches are consistently hitting fifty-five. One of them blows us all away and hits sixty.

"Did you see that?" Donnie asks. "Did you see that pitch?"

I nod.

"That will do the job," he says. "That will beat the Beast. But you've got to throw it every time."

"I don't think I can throw it every time," I say.

"Then you need to do some more push-ups," he says. "And crunches. Drop and give me fifty."

I sigh, but I do as told. A few feet away, my catchers (Aubree and Hannah) follow my lead. Donnie has only been working with us for two days, but we've already learned the drill.

By the end of practice, I still can't hit sixty miles per hour consistently, but I'm getting there. It's not uncommon for me to hit fifty-eight, and I never drop below fifty-five.

"Not bad," Donnie says. "Not bad at all. You keep working this hard, and you'll be pitching for me at Western one day."

"Really?" I ask. I'm in complete shock. I've always wanted to go to college, but I never pictured I'd go as a softball player.

"Anything is possible," Donnie says. "If you work hard."

Chapter 18

Our tournament today is here in our hometown, Everett, which is about twenty minutes north of Seattle. It's at Kasch Park, which is a small but nice park on the west side of town, not too far from Boeing's main aircraft plant. On the way to the game, we drive past the main building, and I never fail to be amazed at the size of that beast. Someone once told me it's the largest building in the world, and I believe it, since it seems to stretch on forever.

Anyway, we're all pretty excited, since we've been working so hard these past two weeks with Steven and Donnie and we want to see how much we've improved, but we're a little apprehensive, too, since the ending of our last game was so traumatic, with the big showdown and loss to Mr. Moran. We're all relieved when we arrive at the field and look at the list of teams participating in this tournament, and we see the Beast are not listed. We know we're going to have to deal with them eventually, but at least we don't have to do it today. Today we can just have fun and do our best.

Payton seems a little gun shy at first, and she's still slightly traumatized by the last game, but she gets over it quickly. Our first game is against another local team called the Snohomish Stars, and Payton leads the way with a perfect 4-4 day. She gets three singles and a double. We win 6-2.

The only bad thing about this tournament, however, is we don't have Kaitlin. Her team, the Washington Wildcats, is in Las Vegas, so she can't play with us this weekend. So I have to pitch every game, but I actually don't mind, because I'm curious to see if my work with Donnie has paid any dividends.

Trust me, it has. During the first game, against the Shock, I'm okay, but it's our second game, against a team called the Lake Stevens Lasers, where I start to really notice a difference. I start to really focus on my snaps, and I try to get them as perfect as possible, and my velocity climbs. At one point, I'm throwing so hard I'm actually overwhelming the Laser batters. I strike out five girls in a row, which is something I've never done before.

I'm actually a little disappointed, however, because Donnie isn't here to see it. Unfortunately, he had an event scheduled with his team at Western Washington.

The second game is a total success, as is the one after it. I strike out ten batters in the second game, and twelve in the third. Everyone is impressed. Especially James.

"Wow," he says. "That was impressive. That was the best I've ever seen you throw. By far."

"Thanks," I say.

Things get even better during our end-of-the-day postgame meeting.

"I was reading a little more in my coaching manuals," James says. "And I found something some coaches do I thought was pretty neat, so I'm going to start doing it, too. After each day of play, I'm going to award a game ball, or game balls if appropriate, to a player I think did an outstanding job that day.

Today, I think everyone did great, but I think two players were absolutely stunning. The first was Payton. Four hits in the first game, three in the second, and a solo home run in the final. It doesn't get much better than that."

We all cheer as he hands her a shiny, new ball. On one of its sides he's written 'Game Ball' and included the date below it.

"The second game ball," he says. "Goes to Paige. She pitched three straight games and only gave up six hits, two in each game. In addition, in the last game, she struck out every batter in their lineup at least once. There's only one way to describe her fastball today — wicked."

Everyone cheers, and I'm nothing but smiles. I can hardly begin to explain how happy getting that game ball made me feel. To be honest, I don't really care about the ball itself (I'll probably just throw it in the closet when I get home), but what it stands for means everything to me. I worked harder than ever during these past two weeks, and it paid off. What a wonderful feeling that is. It's a complete high.

Afterward, when no one is looking, I drop to the ground and do fifty push-ups and crunches.

I know it may sound silly, but this system of Donnie's is working, so I'm sticking with it.

The next day is more of the same. Our first game is against a team from Bainbridge Island called the Islanders. Now, I don't mean to be too critical, and it's not really my place to judge other teams' names, but Bainbridge Island Islanders? How uncreative and redundant is that? What are they going to do next? Form a team from Seattle called the Seattle Seattleites? Or one from Washington called the

Washington Washingtonians? It's really silly, if you ask me.

At the same time, however, I have to give the Islanders credit. They're a good team, and they give us a run for the money. I pitch well, but their batters are much better than the ones I faced the day before, so I only get five strikeouts. In the meantime, I give up six hits, including a double in the fifth that scores two runs.

Luckily for me, however, I'm not the only player who has been working hard lately, and my teammates come to my aid. Payton, like always, is awesome, and she hits a massive home run in the fourth. But the rest of the girls bat nearly as well (clearly their work with Steven is helping them as much as my work with Donnie is helping me), and they attack the Islanders' pitcher with a vengeance. Madison gets two singles, Jennie gets a single and a double, Kaya gets a triple, and Aubree hits her first home run ever. It's a massive shot to straightaway center, and it completely finishes the Islanders off. The final score is 5-3.

Our second game is against the Portland Pioneers (for a team from Oregon, we certainly see them a lot), and it's not nearly as dramatic as our game against the Islanders. Kaya gets us rolling in the first inning with a double that scores Payton and Madison, and we never look back from there. My pitching is solid, and I strike out seven. We win 4-0.

As the game ends, we all look around at each other, and we can hardly believe it. For the first time ever, we've reached the championship game. And if we win the championship game, we will have won our first title ever.

As you can imagine, we're pretty nervous, especially at first. Payton is fine, since she's played in a lot of championship games before, but for the rest of us, it's a completely new experience. Even James is nervous, since he's never coached in a championship game before. So we struggle during the first two innings, and we quickly give up two runs, but Payton keeps us as calm and as reassured as possible.

"Don't worry," she says. "We'll get the runs back. We've just got to have faith."

The game is against a team called the Seattle Sparks, and they're really good. I know from the start I'm going to have to be really sharp, and really focus on my snaps, but at the same time, I'm not overly worried. Despite my nervousness, my confidence, both in myself and my teammates, is at an all-time high.

It's an epic battle. The Sparks lead until the third, when Emily hits a double that scores Payton and Madison. The score remains tied until the fifth, when the Sparks' catcher hits a solo home run off of me. At first I'm a little disappointed, since I gave up a home run, but I have to give the batter credit. I made a good pitch, but she did a great job and hit it a mile.

The Sparks stay in front until the final inning, when Payton launches a two-run home run to left center.

With that shot, we win 4-3.

The celebration afterward is awesome. The tournament director is a man named Steven Shields, and he gives the Sparks a second-place ribbon, then comes over and gives us the championship trophy, which is huge and shaped like a sparkling, golden cup. He also gives us championship T-shirts, and to be perfectly honest I actually like the T-shirts better than the trophy. We slip them on and everyone takes pictures of us, both as a group and as individuals. At one point we take some really silly ones, including one where Payton and I are kissing the trophy at the same time from opposite sides, and another is of Aubree strumming the trophy like it's an electric guitar. The best photo, however, is of James. He's holding the trophy in his hands, and he's tipping it back, like he's drinking champagne out of it. He's smiling brightly, and it's the happiest I've ever seen him. Ten minutes later, he awards the day's game ball, and we all cheer as Aubree wins it.

But the championship presentation isn't the end of the day's fun. About twenty minutes later, as I'm doing my push-ups (it's my new routine, I do fifty push-ups and crunches after every game), I hear James, standing about twenty feet away, talking to a young, attractive woman. She's clearly a reporter of some type, because she has a notepad in one hand.

"My name is Wendy Glavine," she says. "I'm from the Herald. I normally cover the local high school games, but my editor wanted something a little different for tomorrow's paper. There are rumors going around town there is a new team that was formed by Judge Wilson as some sort of punishment."

James nods. "That's us," he says. "Some of the girls got in trouble for drinking, and Judge Wilson wanted to keep them out of any additional trouble, so he made them join a team. It keeps them busy."

"Really?" Wendy asks. Her eyes are large with interest. "Has it been a success?"

James laughs. "I'd say so," he says. "None of the girls have been in any trouble since, at least as far as I know, and we just won this trophy, so I'd say we're doing pretty well."

He holds up our trophy so she can see it.

"This is exactly the type of story I'm looking for," she says. "Our readers will eat it up. Do you mind if I follow up? Can I speak to some of your girls?"

I smile. I've never thought of myself as one of James's girls before. In a strange sort of way, however, I like it. I can't exactly explain why, but I do.

"Feel free," he says. He points at me. "Paige is right over there. She's our star pitcher."

Five minutes later, I'm being interviewed. It's great fun, and it's arguably the most attention I've ever gotten.

It's amazing how much life can change in so short a period of time. Two months ago, I was bored out of my mind, drinking alcohol with boys, and facing thirty days in the detention center as a result. Now, I'm a star pitcher (according to James), I've got a championship T-shirt, and I'm going to be in the newspaper tomorrow.

It's awesome.

Chapter 19

I can hardly believe it, but we're famous. Wendy's article came out in the newspaper on Monday, and it created quite a buzz around town. A day after that, at our practice, a news truck rolled up, with a reporter and a camera crew inside. That night, we were on television. They interviewed several of us, and it was great fun. The only bad thing was my hair looked terrible, since they showed up unexpectedly and I didn't have any time to do anything with it, but even so it was still fun to watch (I've never been on tv before). My dad was so proud he called my grandparents in Spokane and told them all about it.

That night, my Facebook and Twitter accounts went crazy. Within an hour of the tv interview, I received 3,421 friend requests, and I spent the entire rest of the night responding to tweets from new fans. At first it was great fun, but after awhile I started to get pretty frustrated, because in the time it took me to respond to one tweet, four more would come in. My fingers actually started to get cramps from typing so much.

It isn't easy being a star.

Life gets even better at our practice on Thursday. James gathers us up and announces our next tournament is in Wenatchee, a small city about four hours east of Seattle.

"A road trip?" Madison asks. "Awesome. I've never been on a road trip before."

None of us (other than Payton) have, so we're all pretty excited. But then reality sets in.

"Aren't road trips expensive?" Jennie asks. "How are we going to afford it?"

"Don't we have to get a hotel for the night?" Aubree asks.

"My parents can't afford a hotel," Kaya says.

"My parents can't afford anything," Emily says.

James smiles. "You don't need to worry about that," he says. "We have plenty of money."

"What do you mean?" I ask. "Did Judge Wilson give us some more money?"

James shakes his head. "No," he says. "But someone else did."

"We have a sponsor?" Payton asks. Her eyes are big and hopeful.

"No," James says. "We don't have a sponsor. We have five sponsors."

He puts special emphasis on the word five.

We all sit there in complete shock. We don't really know what to say. Five sponsors?

"Apparently," James says, "people all around town love your story. A bunch of misfits gone good. They're eating it up. Everyone wants to be a part of it. I spent all day yesterday handling the details. Take a look at these checks."

He hands us five checks. One is from Boeing. Another is from Microsoft. A third is from Amazon. Two more are from companies I don't recognize.

The amounts on the checks are staggering. I've never seen that much money in my entire life.

"With these checks," James says, "our trip to Wenatchee is covered. Your parents won't have to pay a thing. But you'll still need to get their permission. And I'll need a couple of moms to come as chaperones. Do me a favor and see if any of them are willing to do it."

At this point, I'm so excited I'll force my mom to come, if that's what it takes. I want to do a road trip. It sounds like great fun.

"There's one more thing," James says. "I ran the idea by Judge Wilson, to make certain he was okay with it, and he said it was a great idea."

"Will Kaitlin be coming with us?" I ask.

James smiles. "She will," he says.

We cheer. Technically, Kaitlin is only a pick-up player, but as far as we're concerned she's a member of the team, so we want her with us whenever possible.

"It gets even better," James says. "Judge Wilson thinks this may be the first of many road trips for the Missfits, but he doesn't think it's appropriate for girls to go on a road trip with only one set of uniforms. Especially a road trip like this one, east of the mountains where it's so hot and we may not be able to launder our gear easily, like we do here at home. So he sent this."

He hands us a large cardboard box. Inside is a whole new set of uniforms, one for each of us. They're similar to our original jerseys, but they're white, with navy and gold lettering (our original jerseys were the reverse, navy with white and gold lettering).

When I get home, I spend an hour standing in front of my mirror. First I put on my new white jersey, then I put on my original navy one. They both look like a million bucks.

I can't wait 'til Wenatchee.

Chapter 20

Road trips rule. We take four different cars, with three or four girls in each car, plus an assortment of parents, including several moms who are serving as chaperones. Madison, Aubree, and I ride with James in his Escalade, which is totally awesome. Originally, I get to sit in the front passenger seat, next to James as he drives, so I think I'm the queen of the world, but Madison forces me to switch seats with her when we stop for gas in a city called Leavenworth. Regardless, I'm not disappointed for long, and we rock out to music (the Escalade has an awesome stereo), and James gets us a bunch of goodies from the gas station. We spend about twenty minutes debating which M&M's are the best, and we come to a general consensus that it's either coconut or peanut butter, and we all agree the mint ones are terrible.

We arrive in Wenatchee around 6:00 pm, and it's pretty much like all cities in eastern Washington: small, dusty, and hot. We check into our hotel, which is quite nice, and drop our stuff off in our rooms. We have four girls per room, and I'm sharing a room with Madison, Aubree, and Kaya. After making ourselves at home, we head to the most important place in the hotel:

The pool.

It just doesn't get much better than that. A pool, in the middle of summer, on a softball trip. I should have thought of this years ago.

We spend an hour in the pool, and then fifteen minutes in the adjacent hottub, then James comes down and rounds us up for dinner. We take a vote and decide to go to a local steakhouse called, appropriately, *The Steakhouse*. It's really good, and the garlic mashed potatoes are to die for. I ask for a second serving.

But after dinner, once we've returned to our rooms for the night, something unexpected, and quite unpleasant, happens.

I'm laying on the bed, flipping channels on tv, trying to recover from dinner (my stomach is so full of mashed potatoes I think it's going to burst), when Madison digs through her softball bag and pulls out something for all of us to see.

"Are you guys ready for some real fun?" she asks.

She has a large smile on her face.

Our eyes get big as we see what she's holding.

It's a bottle of tequila.

"Where did you get that?" Kaya asks.

"From some kids at school," Madison says. "And they gave me a great deal on it."

At first, I don't know what to do. I look quickly from face to face, to see how the other girls are reacting. Madison looks excited, but Kaya and Jennie look exactly the same as me — alarmed and nervous.

"You can't have that here," I say.

"Don't worry," Madison says. "No one will know. We can hide it in the closet, where no one can find it. And we can help ourselves to it whenever we're in the mood. Look, I even brought some cups."

She reaches into her bag and pulls out a small, unopened bag of red Solo cups.

"I don't want that in our room," Jennie says.

"Me, neither," Kaya says. "That's what got us in trouble in the first place. Three times. And we nearly spent a month in the detention center as a result."

"It's no big deal," Madison says.

"Yes it is," I say. "If something happens, and Judge Wilson finds out about this, he'll crucify us. This team is our last chance."

"He won't find out," Madison says.

"That's what you said last time," Jennie says. "And the time before that. And we got caught each time. Remember?"

"That's because we were at a party," Madison says. "And everyone was being too loud. The police were bound to show up eventually. But here we'll keep it quiet. On the low. Just the four of us will know about it. Plus Payton if she decides to join us."

My heart races. "You told Payton?" I ask.

"Yeah," Madison says. "I told her to come over and join us, but she didn't look too excited. I think she may be one of those up-and-up types. Oh well. Her loss. Our gain."

"No it isn't," I say. "I want you to get rid of that bottle immediately. Dump it down the drain, or take it out and throw it in the dumpster or something."

"No way," Madison says. "This is some good stuff. I'm not going to waste it like that."

"I don't want it here," I say. "I don't want to take any chances. This softball team is the best thing to happen to me in a long time. It's a lot of work, there's no doubt about it, but it's worth it. I've never felt as good as I have these past few months. And Judge Wilson was right — the only reason we were going to parties and drinking that stuff in the first place was because we were bored and had nothing else to do. If he finds out we're drinking again, who knows what he'll do. He may disband the team and throw us in the detention center."

There is a long, awkward silence as we all stand there, waiting for something to happen. For a minute, I think we're at a complete standstill, and Madison won't budge. But then, after what seems like an eternity, Kaya and Jennie come to my aid.

"I agree with Paige," Kaya says. "I like this team. I never got to go on a road trip before, and I'd like to go on more in the future. So I'm not going to do anything to jeopardize it."

"And I like winning trophies," Jennie says. "So I'm not going to jeopardize it either. Get rid of the alcohol, Madison."

Her face is completely stern, and to be honest, I don't think I've ever seen her so serious before.

"Or what?" Madison asks.

"Or I'll take it from you," Jennie says, "and I'll dump it down the toilet myself."

Madison's face gets really red, and she won't speak to the rest of us for the remainder of the night, but she does as told. She opens the bottle and pours it down the bathroom sink.

Twenty minutes later, as I climb into bed, I have mixed feelings. I don't like the fact we made Madison mad, but at the same time, I know we made the right decision. Alcohol is a thing of our past. And it's going to stay where it belongs — in the past. From this point forward, we're softball players.

Chapter 21

This is easily the largest tournament we've competed in. It's called the Wenatchee Invite, and it features fifty teams from all over the Pacific Northwest. Our first game is at 9:00 am and is against a team from Boise called the Broncos. The Broncos wear fancy, blue uniforms, but they're nothing compared to our new white ones. We look awesome, and we're all glad to be wearing white, since it's eighty degrees by the time we start the game. At first I'm concerned about the heat, since we've rarely played in these conditions before, but it doesn't faze us at all. Payton and Kaitlin start a hit parade in the third inning, and before I know it, we're cruising to an easy 6-1 win. I pitch well, and I finish the game with seven strikeouts and only one walk.

Our next game isn't quite as easy. It's against the Portland Pioneers (we've played them so many times now I'm getting sick of seeing them), and it's a good battle. Kaitlin pitches, and she gives up three runs in the first inning, but then settles down and cruises from there. It takes us awhile to get our bats going, but once we do, there's no stopping them. We explode for seven runs in the fifth, and get three more in the sixth. The final score is 10-3. We're all smiles as we pack up our stuff and switch fields for our final game of the day.

Well, we're all smiles except one.

Madison.

She hasn't said a thing all day. She's still upset about the night before, and she's still mad we made her dump her tequila down the sink. But, much to our delight, her attitude changes completely in the final game.

Our final game is against a team from Montana called the Mountaineers. They're really good. Every player on the team is huge, and they all swing their bats like they know what they're doing. I pitch well, but they really make we work for each out. As we head into the seventh inning, the score is tied 6-6.

The Mountaineers get the first two outs (I'm one of them, ugh), but then Kaitlin gives us hope by hitting a single. It's just a blooper, just out of the reach of the Mountaineers' third baseman, but we'll take it anyway. Payton follows with another single, and Kaitlin races all of the way to third (she is so fast it's amazing). Madison is the next batter, and James calls a timeout to speak with her briefly.

"Here's your chance," he says. "Two outs in the bottom of the seventh. Runners on first and third. A base hit wins it for us. Time for you to be the hero, Madison."

She walks over to the batter's box and digs her cleats into the dirt. She taps her bat on the plate. She looks nervous, but excited at the same time. The first pitch is down and away for a ball. The second is up and in. She swings and misses it badly. She takes a breath, then tries again, but the next pitch blows by her so fast she doesn't even have a chance to swing at it.

She takes a brief timeout, then steps back into the box. She's got a tinge of fear in her eyes, but with that fear, there is determination, too. Madison has always been a tough cookie, as long as I've known her, and she never goes down without a fight. The next pitch is a wicked curveball, one of the nastiest I've ever seen, but it doesn't fool her for a second. She waits until the last second, then hammers it to right field.

As such, we win 7-6. Everyone goes crazy, and we run onto the field and tackle Madison right there on the spot, right as she steps on first base. It's a great pigpile, and everyone jumps on top. At one point, I've got Payton on top of me, and Aubree beneath me, and someone else's knee is in my side. It's somewhat painful, but I don't care, because it's so much fun.

The best part, however, comes a few minutes later, just after we round up our stuff and are carrying it to the adjacent parking lot. Madison walks up to me from behind.

"You're right," she says.

"Excuse me?" I say.

"You're right," she says. "Softball is better than alcohol. Way better."

She walks off with a smile on her face.

Chapter 22

The next day is more softball action. Our first game is against a team from Yakima called the Dust Devils. They're pretty good, and they're a serious challenge until the fourth inning, when Aubree hits a massive grand slam (Madison, Jennie, and I are on base when she does it). The final score is 6-4. Kaitlin pitches and, like always, is stellar.

The next game, however, is a struggle from the start. It's against a really good team called the Seattle Sky. They're unforgettable because they have a mascot named Homer, and he's the cutest chocolate Labrador puppy you have ever seen. He has deep, brown hair and sparkling eyes. Like most Labradors, he loves everybody, especially softball girls, and he doesn't care if you're on his team or not. If you're in a softball uniform, you're his friend. He comes out to meet us before the game and he gives everyone a kiss. Madison gets a particularly wet one right across the side of her face. The umpires love Homer, too, because during games, he fetches foul balls that fly into the parking lots and brings them back for them.

"We need to be really sharp this game," Kaitlin warns us. "This is one of the best teams in the state. Even my Wildcats team struggles against them."

She isn't kidding. Their first batter is a girl named Angel Williams, and she hits my first pitch off of the outfield fence for a stand-up double. The next batter does the same.

I can hardly believe it. After just two pitches, we're losing 1-0.

From that point forward, things get a little better, but not much. The Sky get at least one run in every inning, and by the fifth inning they are leading 6-0. I get a little redemption in the bottom of the fifth when I hit a triple that scores Aubree from first. We get one more run in the bottom of the sixth when Payton hits a solo home run, but that's the best we can do. We end up losing 6-2.

With the loss, our tournament is officially over. But to be honest, we're not too disappointed, since 4-1 is still a pretty good record for a team making its first road trip ever. Kaitlin tells us when she went on her first road trip, with her first team (the Khaos), they didn't win a single game.

We stop at Sonic on the way out of town, and James buys everyone dinner, and I gorge myself on a chili cheeseburger with fries and a large chocolate shake. The drive home is fun, and we rock out for awhile, but after about an hour everyone gets pretty tired, and before I know it we girls are all asleep.

Chapter 23

It's amazing. Every day seems to get a little better for us. Today, James shows up at practice and tells us all to load into his Escalade. It's quite a squeeze, but somehow we all do it.

"Aren't we going to practice?" I ask.

James nods. "Yeah," he says. "But we picked up a new sponsor yesterday, so now we've got a few more options when it comes to practices."

We don't really know what he's talking about, but we figure it out soon enough, as he pulls the Escalade into the parking lot of a large athletic club called, appropriately, *The Players' Club*. It's a converted warehouse, so it's not too fancy on the outside, but inside it's amazing. It has batting cages, pitching machines, weight lifting equipment, free weights, and a bunch of stuff I don't even recognize. As soon as we enter, a man comes out and introduces himself. His name is Steve Logan, and he has a thick Australian accent, and he's super friendly. He treats us like we're royalty, and he shows us all around the facility, and tells us we're free to use any of the equipment we'd like. So we do. Within twenty minutes, we've split up into groups, with some of us are using the pitching machines, others using the cages doing various drills with James, and I'm in a cage with Donnie. He showed up a few minutes after we got here.

"Look at all that weight lifting equipment," he says. "A girl like you could really buff out using all of that equipment."

"I don't need equipment like that," I say.

"Really?" he asks. "Why is that?"

"Because," I say. "Real pitchers don't use equipment. Instead, they do push-ups and crunches."

His smile is huge. "Good girl," he says. "Good girl indeed. Now drop and give me fifty."

Our pitching lesson today is great. Donnie decides it's time I spend some time working on my 'other' pitches, meaning my curveball, changeup, and screw.

"Your fastball is awesome," he says. "Your improvement is remarkable. But when you face the really good teams, like the Wildcats, Beast, and Sky, it's not going to be enough."

I think back to the game against the Seattle Sky, and I have no choice but to agree.

"So we've got to master at least two more pitches," he says. "Ideally three."

From there we go to work. He doesn't like my screwball at all, claiming I'm gripping the ball wrong, so we start at square one. It's a little frustrating at first, and my first ten pitches fly all over the place, but, like always, Donnie knows what he's doing and is eventually able to coax some serious improvement out of me. It'll be awhile before I have it mastered, but I'm off to a good start.

The only bad part of practice is Payton. Like always, Steven works with her, and he constantly tries to help her learn how to hit changeups, but it's absolutely hopeless. She cannot hit a changeup to save her life. After awhile, even Donnie heads over, and he tries to help her too, but his advice is as worthless as Steven's. Finally, Payton gets so frustrated she throws her bat down and stomps into the locker room with tears running down her cheeks.

"I don't know what to do," Steven says. "I've tried everything. I've never seen a girl, especially a girl as good as her, struggle so much."

"Just keep trying," Donnie says. "She'll figure it out eventually. I hope."

Chapter 24

Today is a great day at school (you won't hear me say that very often). I'm in gym class, and we're having some sort of fitness test where we have to do all kinds of exercises, like running the hundred meter dash, running the mile, bench press, pull ups, etc. Most of it is pretty boring and routine, and I hate the running drills (especially the mile, it nearly kills me and I get a terrible time), but everything changes when our teacher, Ms. Johns, announces the next drill is push-ups. Everyone forms a line, and I'm the last person to go. Apparently, we saved the best for last, for I destroy the school's record for girls, and I do more push-ups than every boy in the class except one, but he's a star player on the school's football team, so he doesn't count. At one point, as I'm doing my push-ups, everyone in the class starts cheering and clapping, and no one can believe how many I'm capable of doing.

When I've finished, several classmates ask me how I was able to do so many, and my response is a simple one.

"Donnie," I say.

The same thing happens when we do crunches. I set both school records (for boys and girls), and I beat everyone in the class, including the boy (Liam Tyler) from the football team.

Ms. Johns looks at me with a smile on her face. "One thing is for sure," she says. "That performance will get you an A."

After that, it gets even better. A classmate of mine (her name is Janey Levine — she's a great volleyball player), points at my arms.

"No wonder you can do so many push-ups," she says. "Look at those guns. You're ripped."

"You're a beast," another classmate says.

"Incredible," Liam says.

I look down at my arms, and I realize they're right. Normally I wear a T-shirt in gym class, but today I wore a tank top, so my arms are fully exposed, and it's true. They're nothing but muscle. I've never seen my biceps so well developed, and my triceps are absolutely huge. What a difference. Two months ago, my triceps were so small I didn't even know they existed.

"You better be careful," Janey says. "If you get too big, you may scare the boys away. I hear they don't like it if a girl is stronger than them."

I laugh. "If a boy doesn't like me because I'm too strong," I say. "Then he isn't worth my time."

Everyone laughs.

"Good for you, Paige," Ms. Johns says.

Apparently, however, Liam is the type of boy who likes strong girls. He waits several minutes, until mostly everyone has wandered off to other parts of the gym, then walks up to me and asks if I'd like to go to dinner with him after school today. I'm totally caught off guard, because Liam is one of the most popular boys at school, and he's really cute, and he's never really talked to me before.

But apparently I finally caught his eye, and, as such, we're off to dinner.

Chapter 25

"You lucky dog," Madison says. "How did you do it?"

We're all at practice, at *The Players' Club*, and we're supposed to be doing our warm-up stretches and drills, but the other girls are more interested in the details of my date with Liam.

"I didn't do a thing," I say. "He asked me out. Totally out of the blue. I never saw it coming."

"Where did you go?" Jennie asks.

"Roberto's," I say. Roberto's is a small, family-owned pizza place right across from my school.

"I love that place," Kaya says.

"Who cares about the place?" Aubree says. "How was the date? What did you do?"

"It was nothing fancy," I say. "We went right after school, so I didn't really have time to change into anything nice or whatever, and we just ordered a pizza and talked."

"What about?" Madison asks.

"This and that," I say. "He's really nice. He's originally from Portland, but his parents moved to Everett when he was four. His dad owns some type of construction company on the waterfront. They have a house on the north side of town, on Grand."

"A house?" Madison says. "Have you ever seen it? It's a block from my cousin's house. It's not a house. It's a mansion."

"What's he like?" Aubree asks.

"Really nice," I say. "He's got two younger brothers, but I forget their names. I kept getting distracted every time he would look at me."

"I know," Jennie says. "He has the most gorgeous eyes. They're like ice blue."

"Totally," Madison says.

"Are you going out again?" Aubree asks.

"Yeah," I say. "Friday night. And then he said he's going to come to our tournament this weekend. And he said he might bring some of his friends, some other guys from the football team, so we need to put on a good show."

"You don't need to worry about that," Aubree says. "If football players are coming, we will."

At that point, we all return to practice, and I notice everyone's effort is even better than normal. Apparently, the thought of a bunch of cute football players coming to our game is good motivation indeed.

Chapter 26

Our tournament today is in Seattle, at Lower Woodland Park, which is right next to Green Lake, an old but really cute part of town. The weather is nice, and we're all in a good mood, but we're a little nervous, too, because we want to impress Liam and his football friends (the other girls are hoping they can meet some of them between games). I'm in a really good mood, because Liam and I had our date the night before, and it was really fun. He took me to dinner and a movie, and I had a great time.

Our first game is against (who else?) the Portland Pioneers. I wonder if they ever play games in Oregon, because they're always up here in Washington. Regardless, we get off to a good start, and we take the lead in the bottom of the fourth inning when Payton hits a two-run home run. My pitching is really good, and I try out some of the new pitches I've been working on with Donnie, and they're a nice complement to my fastball. My screwball isn't great, but my curveball and changeup are nasty at times, and in the end I strike out nine batters. We win, and the final score is 5-1.

As expected, we sneak off between games, when we have a break, and we meet up with Liam and his friends. Everyone hits it off really well, and we all get goodies from a nearby concession stand. Liam's friends compliment us on a great game, but I'm not too concerned about them right now. I just want to know what Liam thought.

"Wow," he says. "How do you throw so hard? Those batters didn't have a chance."

I shrug. I'm tempted to brag a little, but I decide it would be better to be humble.

Boys like humble, right?

"Just doing my job," I say.

"Well keep doing it," he says. "You're awesome."

I'm nearly floating on air as I head to our next game. I cannot believe how good I feel. But things get even better when Jennie runs up to me as we're warming up.

"He's crazy about you," she says.

"How do you know?" I ask.

"I can see it in his eyes," she says. "And look. His buddies are teasing him right now. They can tell, too."

We look across the field, to the boys, and see them sitting in a group in the bleachers. From where we're standing, we can't hear what they're saying, but it's clear they're joking around and teasing Liam. In the meantime, he's all smiles.

It's amazing how well I can pitch when I'm on top of the world. Our next game is against a team called the Edmonds Express. They're a good team, but they're no match for me, and I strike out batter after batter (I'm pitching every game this weekend because Kaitlin is with the Wildcats in Los Angeles). The game goes by so quickly I hardly even realize when we reach the final inning.

But then something unexpected happens. James walks up to me, and he has a strange look on his face.

"I probably shouldn't tell you this," he says. "Because it'll jinx you, but you're three outs away from a perfect game."

Every head in the dugout turns to look at me.

I can hardly believe it. A perfect game is the holy grail of softball. It's when a pitcher throws an entire game and never lets a single batter reach first base. It's even better than a no-hitter. It's rarely done, by any pitcher, at any level.

Wouldn't that be something? What if I could pitch a perfect game, right now, in front of Liam? If that didn't impress him, nothing would.

As I walk back onto the field, I realize something has happened. Word has spread, and fans from all over the park, including people who were watching other games on other fields, have wandered over to see if I can do the impossible.

"You can do it," Liam shouts from the bleachers.

Clearly, he and the other boys realize what's at stake, too.

For the first time all day, I feel nervous. Big time. So many people have wandered over that the bleachers are now completely filled, and there are even people standing along the first and third base foul lines. I've never played in front of this many people before, and I'm starting to feel the heat.

Clearly the pressure gets to me, for my first two pitches are off target, for balls, but the batter bails me out by hitting a weak grounder to third. Jennie grabs it and whips it to first for the initial out.

I take a big breath.

One down, two to go.

The next batter puts up a fight by fouling off three of my pitches in a row, but then she hits a lazy fly ball to center. Payton catches it for out number two.

I can hardly believe it.

Two down, one to go.

Now I'm really feeling the pressure. I'm so close I can taste it. The crowd is already cheering, and they want to see me do it. Liam and the boys are chanting my name repeatedly.

But there's one problem. The Express' next batter is their best batter. She's a big blonde named Amy Allison, a power-hitting lefty, so I know it's not going to be easy to get her out.

Much to my surprise and delight, however, it is. She hits my very first pitch straight back at me. Without even thinking, I stick up my glove, and the ball flies right into it.

"It's a catch," the umpire yells. "The game is over. Congratulations, young lady."

The next few minutes are crazy. The audience cheers, Liam and the boys go wild, and my teammates lift me high into the air and carry me around the infield like I'm some kind of fancy trophy.

Some days, life is good.

Real good.

Today is one of them.

Chapter 27

Today is the beginning of our second road trip of the season, and this is a really good one. We're heading north for the weekend to Vancouver, British Columbia. It takes about two hours to get to the Canadian border, then an hour to get through the border, then an hour to get to downtown Vancouver. It's been about five years since my last visit (my family did a weekend trip), but the city is pretty much as I remember: gorgeous. The downtown area sits right on the water, with snow-capped mountains in the distant background. In many ways it reminds me of Seattle, but without the Space Needle, of course.

Our hotel is in an area north of downtown, just across the bay. Like always, we check in, dump our stuff in our rooms, then head straight for the pool. After an hour of fun and frolicking, we head to dinner, which is always fun. Everyone is in a good mood and excited about the tournament, but James gives us a few warnings.

"I picked this tournament for several reasons," he says. "One, I thought it would be good fun, since Vancouver is a great place. But even more important, our season is starting to wind down, and we've only got a few more tournaments left."

We all boo. We don't like the sound of that at all.

"The biggest tournament of all," James says, "is Western Nationals. It's the most prestigious we've participated in so far. It's coming up in three weeks, and I want us primed and ready for it. So I want us to play some really tough competition in the meantime, to get us ready for it, and from what I hear, these Canadian teams are as tough as they get."

"Sweet," I say. "I'm up for the challenge."

"Me, too," Madison says.

"That's what I wanted to hear," James says. "I think you'll do fine."

Our food arrives, and the conversation dies off for a few minutes as we dig in, but finally Madison brings up a topic that has been on a lot of our minds lately.

"What's going to happen," she asks, "when the season ends?"

James smiles. "I wondered when someone was going to ask me about that," he says. "Judge Wilson and I were discussing it just the other day."

He turns to Judge Wilson, who is sitting to his right, devouring a piece of roasted chicken.

"Do you want to take it from here?" James asks.

Judge Wilson sets his fork down and addresses us. "The next step is up to you ladies," he says. "As far as I'm concerned, you've done an exemplary job. You've played great and stayed out of trouble. As such, at the end of the season, I'm releasing you from your sentence, and you can do whatever you'd like. But please do me a favor and stay out of my courtroom from now on."

We smile. None of us have any problems with that. As far as I'm concerned, I'm never going back to that courtroom again. Except maybe to say hi to Judge Wilson.

"That's not what I meant," Madison says. "What's going to happen with the team? At the end of the season, are you going to shut the Missfits down for good? Or will there be a team next year?"

Judge Wilson smiles. "Next year?" he asks. "None of you seemed excited about my idea when I first proposed it. I assumed you would play for one year, then call it good."

For a brief second, my heart sinks. I've had so much fun playing softball I hate the idea of it coming to an end.

"I'm going to keep playing," Kaya says. "I'll try out for another team if I have to. Maybe Kaitlin's team, the Wildcats, if they have a spot open. But to be honest, I'd prefer to stay on the Missfits."

Judge Wilson smiles. "Really?" he asks. "What about the rest of you? Are you going to keep playing softball?"

I don't even have to think about it.

"I am," I say.

"Me, too," Madison says.

"Me, too," Emily says.

"I'd like to," Aubree says. "But I don't know if my parents can afford it. Especially a fancy team like the Wildcats. They have a team fee, right?"

"Interesting," Judge Wilson says. "How many of you would play for the Missfits again if I reformed the team next year?"

In complete unison, every girl says she would.

"I guess I have no choice," Judge Wilson says. "Like the Phoenix, the Missfits will rise once again."

We cheer. My heart is actually racing in my chest. This is exactly what I've been hoping for for quite awhile now, but I was always too afraid to ask.

"But don't get too excited," Judge Wilson says. "Because there is still one big piece of the puzzle we need to put in place. We still need a coach for next year. James hasn't said he'd do it yet."

We all turn to him, and none of us are above groveling, so we grovel like there is no tomorrow.

"Please James," we say. "We'll do anything."

James smiles. "I'll do it," he says. "But you've got to make me one promise."

"What?" Madison asks.

"Our rematch with the Beast is rapidly approaching," he says. "They're going to be playing in Western Nationals, too, and we're bound to face them sooner or later. I want you all to play the game of your life on that day."

"You've got nothing to worry about," I say. "That's a given."

"We won't let you down," Jennie says.

"Then it's a done deal," he says. "Missfits forever."

We all cheer.

Well, almost everyone cheers. The minute James mentions the name Beast, Payton's eyes grow big, and she sits back in her chair. She doesn't say anything for the remainder of the night.

The next morning, our tournament begins. It's in a beautiful park not too far from our hotel. There are flowers everywhere and you can see the downtown skyscrapers in the background, just across the water. Our first game is against a team called the British Columbia Bearcats, and as James warned us the night before, they are good. Actually, that's an understatement. They're great. The minute I see them, I know there aren't going to be any perfect games today. They're not overly big, but they're lightning fast, great on defense, and solid with their bats. By the third inning, they're leading 3-0.

In the fourth inning, however, something unexpected happens. We all get a reminder that softball isn't all fun and games. I'm pitching, and the batter is the Bearcats' cleanup hitter, a big, power-hitting lefty with dark hair. I throw her a curveball, and she absolutely murders it. She hits it so hard it looks like a blur coming off of her bat. It's a laser line drive, at least a hundred miles an hour, straight at Jennie, who, like usual, is playing third base. Jennie gets her mitt up, but not quite in time. The ball skims off of the top of her mitt, hits her in the side of the neck, and ricochets away. She collapses in a heap. The ball is actually still in play, but the umpire calls the play dead immediately (apparently umpires can stop a play at any time if they feel a player is hurt or in danger of being hurt). Everyone rushes over to help her. By the time we get to her, she's rolling on the ground near third base, clutching her neck, with tears running down her face. James is able to calm her down within a couple of minutes, but she doesn't look good at all, and the entire side of her neck is swollen and bruised. James doesn't want to take any chances, so he has two of our chaperones take her to a local hospital for a check up. Since we're not from around here, we don't know where the nearest hospital is, but the Bearcats' coach and several of their parents come to our aid with an address and directions. One of them even offers to lead them there, just to make certain they find it okay. I'm really impressed. These people have never met us before, but when it comes to the safety and welfare of the players, it doesn't matter what team you are from.

The game resumes about twenty minutes later, and we do okay, but we really have a hard time concentrating. We've never lost a player to injury before, and we're really worried about Jennie. James calls the hospital every twenty minutes, to see how she is doing, and finally we get word she's okay, but even with the good news we don't play with the passion we normally have. The final score is 5-1, and our only run is a solo home run by Payton in the top of the fifth.

Our next two games are a little better, but not much. Our second game is against a team called the Victoria Royals. Like the Bearcats, they are really good. We play well but lose 4-2. Kaitlin pitches fantastic, and our defense is stellar (Kaya makes a diving catch that is so impressive even the other team cheers), but their pitcher is spectacular, and we never really have a chance against her.

Like James said, these teams are good.

Jennie returns to the field in time for the third game. Her neck is swollen, bruised, and wrapped in gauze, but being the trooper she is, she insists on playing. Somewhat reluctantly, James allows her to return to the field, but he puts her in the outfield, where he hopes she will see little action and have a nice, easy, uneventful game.

The game is against a team we've played before, the Boise Broncos. It's a good game, and our spirits are all lifted greatly by Jennie's return. We jump to an early lead when Kaitlin hits a double and Payton follows with a massive home run. She hits it so far it flies over the outfield fence and splashes into a nearby pond, sending a bunch of Canadian geese flying in all directions. Two innings later, she hits another, and we all laugh as one of the geese shoots a nasty glance back at her.

In the meantime, my pitching is solid, and I strike out nine batters, four of them using my new screwball Donnie and I have been working on. The final score is 5-0.

The rest of the evening is good, old-fashioned, road trip fun. We head to dinner, and the girls tease me and congratulate me when I announce that Liam and I are Facebook official. Madison even verifies it by loading Liam's Facebook page on her iPhone. Sure enough, I'm listed as his girlfriend. I get hugs and pats on the back.

We finish the evening by heading to Stanley Park, which is one of the nicest places in the world, at least as far as I'm concerned. It's a gorgeous park in downtown Vancouver right on the water. There are a million things to do (hiking, biking, jogging, splashing in fountains, etc.), but we keep busy by playing a game of cricket with some of the locals. None of us really know how to play, but the local players insist we'll be good at it since we're softball players, so we give it a try. It's a good time. We all look pretty goofy (especially Madison, who can never quite figure out how to hold the cricket bat), but as far as I'm concerned, if you're having fun, goofy is good.

Chapter 28

Today is the second day of our tournament in British Columbia, and it gets off to a good start. The weather is great, and our first game is against a team called the Calgary Cannons. They are solid, but nothing flashy, and they're definitely not as good as the teams we played the day before. Kaitlin pitches and gives up a few runs, but nothing that gives us any real concerns. In the meantime, we play stellar defense, and I have my best day ever at my secondary position, shortstop. At one point, in the third inning, I make all three outs, and later, in the fifth, I make a diving play to rob a batter of a hit. I normally don't like to dive too much, 'cause it hurts, but on occasion you've got to do it, so I do. The only bad thing is I get some nasty grass stains on my uniform, and those are going to take some serious effort to get out.

Anyway, we win 6-3, so we move on to our second game, which is on the same field, so we don't have to move our equipment, which is always nice. The second game is against a local team called the Fraser Valley Vikings. They are really good, and it ends up being a back-and-forth affair. We take the lead in the second inning when Payton and Kaitlin get back-to-back hits, the Vikings tie it up in the fourth when their catcher hits a clutch single, scoring a run, they take the lead in the fifth when a batter hits a solo home run, we tie it up again in the sixth when Zoe,

Aubree, and Hannah get hits, and they come back and win it in the seventh when I walk the leadoff batter (never a good thing to do), and she steals second and scores on two straight sacrifice flies. Zoe's throw to home is close, but the runner is clearly safe.

With the loss, our tournament is officially over. We're a little disappointed, because we wanted to play at least one more game, but at the same time we feel good since our opponents were really tough and we still did fine. As such, we know we'll be ready for our final, ultimate goal in three weeks.

Western Nationals.

The rematch.

Missfits vs Beast.

This time, we will win.

Chapter 29

Today is the day. The day we've waited for all year. The much anticipated battle with the Beast.

The good news is we got Kaitlin for the game, which was a surprise since her team, the Wildcats, has a tournament in Portland, but Kaitlin knew how important this tournament was to us, and especially this game, so she asked her coach for permission to play with us and thankfully he granted it (according to Kaitlin, he's a really nice guy).

As expected, the game is a battle from the start. I've never seen our team so focused on a goal all year. Every girl has one thing and one thing on her mind — winning the game. As such, our effort is amazing, and our caliber of play is the highest it's ever been. Madison makes an amazing running catch to retire a batter in the first inning, Jennie snags a grounder and makes a laser of a throw in the second (I've never seen her throw the ball that hard before), and our middle infielders (Kaitlin and Kaya) turn an amazing double play to end the third inning. In the meantime, I'm throwing the ball with complete conviction, as hard as I can, pitch after pitch. The ball is absolutely exploding as it hits Aubree's mitt.

Despite the effort, however, the Beast keep right with us. They are an amazing team, loaded with talent at every position, and they want the Western Nationals championship, too. They make as many great plays as we do. Their first baseman makes a leaping grab in the first inning, robbing me of a double down the line, their shortstop makes a brilliant throw in the third inning, and their center fielder catches a ball with her back against the wall, stealing a huge hit from Kaitlin in the fourth.

As each inning passes, the pressure starts to mount, and everything gets more and more intense. We all know this game is going to come down to one big play, and we're hoping we're the one to make that play.

Finally, it happens. The game is still scoreless going into the bottom of the seventh inning. It's our turn to bat, so we're feeling pretty good, because we know if we get a run during this inning, we win. But if we don't, we'll go into extra innings. So in a way, we can't really lose, at least for now.

But I am getting a little concerned. I've thrown a ton of pitches already, and I'm covered in sweat (ugh), and I don't know how much longer I can go. My arm, shoulder, and lower back are really starting to hurt. The velocity on my pitches is starting to drop significantly, despite my work with Donnie, and I'm not certain I can aim my pitches as well as I did earlier in the game.

James sees it, too, so he has Kaitlin start to warm up. I know if she comes in, we'll still be in good shape, but regardless, we need to get this game over with as soon as possible.

Unfortunately, the Beast's pitcher, Sydney, gets our first two batters out pretty easily. Payton is our next batter, so normally I would still be happy, because she's so good she can win a game all by herself, but not today.

Today, Payton is a mess. She's been stressed out from the start, nervous and twitchy, and Mr. Moran hasn't helped her any. He's had Sydney throw her nothing but changeups all day, and she's struck out miserably each time. During her last at-bat, she actually managed to foul one pitch away, which was a first for her, but that was the best she could do.

This at-bat appears to be no different. Sydney's first pitch, as expected, is a changeup, and Payton swings at it and misses it terribly. The second pitch is another, and the outcome is the same.

In the distance, in the Beast's dugout, I see Mr. Moran. There is a big smile on his face, and at one point he even pats himself on the knee. He's loving every minute of Payton's agony.

Speaking of Payton, she is hopeless. We can all see it. She takes a practice swing, then takes a big breath, to try to steady herself, then steps back into the batter's box for one last, futile try.

In the meantime, a lone tear runs down her cheek.

"Time," James calls, and he walks toward her. The umpire stops play and sends Payton over to talk to him.

"I'll be the first to admit," James tells her. "I'm not the best coach in the world. And I definitely don't know as much as Donnie and Steven. But I know one thing, Payton. You're an awesome player, and you can hit this next pitch. No offense to our other players, but you're the best player on this team, and everyone knows it. They know you can do it, and I know you can do it, so now it's time you realize it, too. You can do it. Say it."

She looks at him with a puzzled look on her face.

"Say what?" she asks.

"Say you can do it."

She wipes the tear from her cheek with the back of her batting glove.

"I can do it," she says. Her voice is quiet, and there isn't much conviction in it.

"Say it like you mean it," he says.

"I can do it," she says.

"Much better," he says. "Now go do it. And you should be happy right now, Payton. You're about to go over there, to that batter's box, and win us a shiny trophy. You're about to become our biggest hero. A lot of players would kill for that opportunity."

"If you say so," she says.

"No more," he says. "From now on, I only want to hear one thing from your lips. I can do it. Do you hear me?"

"I can do it," she says.

"Good girl," he says. "Now go do it. We all know you can."

He heads back to his spot in the third base coaching box, and she heads, rather slowly, back to the batter's box. I'm not really certain she believes anything James told her, but apparently she's going to give it a try, because I can hear her whispering the words 'I can do it' to herself as she taps her bat on the plate.

"Give her some help," James shouts to us.

From the dugout, we all start to chant, as loudly and as boisterously as we can. "You can do it. You can do it. You can do it."

One pitch later, and much to everyone's delight, she does.

Sydney makes the pitch, and it's one of the nastiest changeups I've ever seen. It's at least twenty miles slower than her normal pitches, probably more.

But for the first time in her life, Payton keeps her chin down, her hands up, and she waits as long as possible. I can see every muscle in her body straining to control itself as the ball heads for the plate.

At the last possible second, she explodes. She hits the ball so hard it flies a mile. The Beast's outfielders don't even try to catch it. They just turn and watch as it flies into the distance. A bunch of little boys chase after it as it lands in an adjacent parking lot.

In the meantime, we go crazy. We charge the field and tackle Payton the minute she steps on home plate. It's an awesome pigpile, and we're all laughing, crying, shouting, and cheering at the same time. At one point, Payton and I hit our helmets together in celebration, and we probably give each other slight concussions, but we don't care, not in the least.

We're Missfits.

We're champions.

As we celebrate, I see Mr. Moran in the Beast's dugout. He's so mad he's throwing bats onto the edge of the field near third base. The umpire is trying to calm him down but he is having little success.

Chapter 30

Today is our end-of-the-season party. It's at Alfy's, a small but nice pizza place not too far from our practice field. It reminds me a lot of our end-of-the-season parties back in Little League. James gives a speech, and it's pretty much the same thing every coach says at the end of the year, but I give him credit because it's his first time giving an end-of-the-season speech, so he'll probably improve in upcoming years.

Judge Wilson is there, too, so he says a few things, about how he's really happy with us for turning our lives around and staying out of trouble. He hopes in the future we can be role models for other girls. He's even thinking about starting a second Missfits team for younger girls next year, either at the 14u or 12u level (he hasn't decided on the specifics yet). He asks us if we'd be willing to help on occasion with the younger girls, and of course we all say yes.

After that, they hand out the season's awards. I win the pitching award (for best pitcher) and Aubree wins the Gold Glove award (for best defender). In the meantime, Payton wins the Silver Slugger award (for best hitter), the team MVP award (for most valuable player), and the coach's award (James's choice). At one point, we tease her and call her an 'award hog.'

As you can probably guess, she's all smiles.

The highlight of the night, however, happens a few minutes later, just before our pizza arrives. James introduces a man named Steven Smith, and we all immediately notice something peculiar about him. He's wearing a polo shirt with the words 'Bellevue Beast' on the chest.

"It's an honor to meet you all," he says. "Thank you for giving me a couple of minutes to speak at your party. I know it's unusual to have someone from another team here, but I appreciate it nonetheless. Anyway, I'm the president of BB LLC, which is the legal entity that owns and controls all of the Bellevue Beast teams, including the 16u team you ladies are so familiar with. I wanted to take a minute to congratulate you on an outstanding season, and on winning the championship at Western Nationals. That was a great game, one for the ages, and I'm sure none of us will ever forget it. That final home run, Payton, was truly amazing. You hit that ball so far, and so high, I think it went into orbit."

We all laugh. It's a good joke, but in reality, we all know what actually happened to the ball. It's in Payton's trophy case at home. After the game, some little boys chased it down, brought it back, and gave it to her as a souvenir.

"But I wanted to come here today," Mr. Smith says, "to talk about something a lot more serious. And something I find quite disturbing. Mr. Moran."

At the mention of his name, the entire room grows deathly silent. You can cut the tension with a butter knife.

"Over the past two seasons," he says, "I've received numerous complaints about Mr. Moran, so I launched an investigation quite awhile ago to verify if the complaints were true. Much to my dismay, they were. As such, I've wanted to fire Mr. Moran for quite some time now, but because of legal concerns, I could not. I had to have all of my ducks in a row before I did anything as drastic as that. James and Judge Wilson will understand my concerns."

Both men smile. Being members of the legal profession, they know exactly what Mr. Smith is talking about.

"Regardless," Mr. Smith says, "I have now completed my investigation, and you will all be happy to hear that I fired Mr. Moran last night. He will never coach another Bellevue Beast team again."

Everyone sits forward in our chairs, and we exchange excited glances. We can hardly believe what we just heard. Can it really be true?

"Now that Mr. Moran is gone," Mr. Smith says, "I am hopeful our two teams, Missfits and Beast, can go back to being friendly rivals. After all, softball is competitive, there's no doubt about that, but ultimately it's supposed to be fun, right? Nobody should leave a game in tears. Isn't that right, Payton?"

She nods.

"Many girls suffered as a result of Mr. Moran's actions," Mr. Smith says. "But none as much as Payton. As such, on behalf of the Beast organization, we apologize, and we want you to know you are welcome to come back to our team, if you'd like. After all, as far as I'm concerned, Payton, you should have never left in the first place."

We all grow instantly alarmed, and we shoot quick glances at Payton. After all we've been through, would she ever consider leaving us and re-joining the Beast? It would break my heart if she did.

Luckily, we have nothing to worry about.

"I'm honored," she tells Mr. Smith. "But the Missfits are my team now, so I'm staying with them."

Mr. Smith smiles. "I had a feeling you'd say that," he says. "Good for you, Payton. Good for all of you. You Missfits are an awesome team, and I really look forward to seeing you again next season on the field. But until then, and once again to make certain there is no bad blood between us, I wanted to tell you I am paying for your dinner tonight. And I brought some friends so we can all celebrate together."

At that, the main door to the restaurant opens, and the entire Beast team enters. At the front is their new coach, a young woman named Kristina Stiles, who looks like she isn't much older than the players themselves. She's soft-spoken and sweet — the exact opposite of Mr. Moran.

The Beast players rush over to Payton, and they give her hugs and pats on the back (they're all friends since they were once teammates), and Sydney apologizes profusely.

"I never wanted to throw those changeups," she says. "I knew it wasn't right, but Mr. Moran was so intimidating."

At one point, she looks like she's about to cry.

"It's okay," Payton says. "It's all behind us now. Now, let's just have some fun."

At that, she formally introduces us to the rest of the Beast players, and they sit down with us (we push several tables together to make room for everyone) and we share stories, and phone numbers, and slices of pizza, and it's great fun. James even makes arrangements with Kristina to play some scrimmage games next spring, and there is talk of us doing a road trip together next year.

"Let's go to Los Angeles," Kaitlin says. "Tournaments in LA are so fun. The fields are great, and then afterward we can go to Newport Beach, and you can all meet my sister if you want, and she can probably get us into a UCLA game for free."

We all like the sound of that. A tournament in LA would be more fun than I can imagine.

Missfits and Beast. Together, we're going to take on the world.

Silence In Center
Preview

Some days suck. May 15, 2013 was one of them. It started off okay but, as was sometimes the case, went downhill fast. I had a tryout with a fastpitch team called the Express, which was a 14u select team from Edmonds, a city about twenty minutes north of Seattle. I was really excited (and a bit nervous) because I had never played select softball before. I had played Little League for three years, and I had made the All-Star team all three years, but I had never tried to move up to the select level until then. The tryout was at a field in downtown Edmonds and it started okay. The team's coaches were nice, but it was still pretty intimidating, especially at first, because there were so many girls there (I'd guess around a hundred total, but there may have been more). The Express was usually a really good team, so a lot of girls wanted to play for them and it was hard to win a spot unless you could really find a way to impress the coaches.

Which, at first, I thought I had done. There were six of them total, and they had us break into groups of ten girls each and go through various drills set up all over the field. My group was led by a coach named James Harbaugh, who was a tall, lean man in his early forties with short, black hair, gray eyes, and a beard. I didn't know it at first, but later found out he was the team's head coach (originally, for some unknown reason, I thought he was one of the assistants). Anyway, he led us to the infield and had us form a single-file line at second base, then hit a series of ground balls to us. Each girl got five, and I fielded each cleanly and whipped it over to first as fast as I could (an assistant was covering the base for us). When we were all done with our grounders, Harbaugh had us jog out to the outfield and he hit fly balls to us. At that point, I was really excited because on my Little League team I was the center fielder so fly balls were my specialty. He hit me three in a row, which I caught easily (on one of them, I didn't even have to move), so then he decided to challenge me a little by hitting one to my left. I had to run about twenty feet to get to it, but I've always been pretty fast (my dad calls me a speedster) so I was able to catch it almost as easily as the first three. Seeing I could catch balls on the run, he decided to really challenge me by hitting one deep into the outfield way over my head. I was forced to run all of the way to the outfield's warning track, and I ended up less than five feet away from the outfield fence itself, but I was able to get to it and make the catch anyway.

At that point, I was as about as happy as I could be. Harbaugh nodded as I made the final catch, and I could tell he was impressed, at least a little. And he wasn't the only one. Sitting in the stands, watching everything intently, was my dad. He was a big sports fan and there was nothing he loved more than watching me play softball, so this was not only a big day for me but for him as well. He really wanted to see me win a spot and begin playing at the select level.

"Way to go, Melody," he called. "Well done."

From there, we moved to an adjacent field and did some hitting drills. Like always, we took turns, and Harbaugh pitched five balls to each of us. There were three girls who went before me, and they all did well. The first girl hit all five pitches sharply, including two that went all of the way to the warning track. The next girl fouled the first pitch away, but then made up for it by hitting the next four straight up the middle. The girl after her hit all five pitches into the outfield, and one of them hit and bounced off of the outfield fence. It was a great hit, and a great overall performance. But it wasn't as good as what I did. I hit my first three pitches straight up the middle, then finished by hitting the final two completely out of the park. The first cleared the fence by about five feet, and the second by about twenty. I was all smiles as I watched the second fly into the distance.

After hitting, Harbaugh got out a stopwatch and timed us running from home plate to first base. My first time was only so-so, but my second time was really good, and I actually got the third best time of the day. As such, as we called it good and wrapped things up, I felt really confident. I felt like I had done everything I could possibly do to make the team, and I felt like I had a legitimate chance of doing so. And I got really excited when my dad and I were walking toward our car in the parking lot and Harbaugh called out to us to wait up for a second. At the beginning of the tryout, he had told us he would not be making any roster decisions for a couple of days, since he liked to mull things over for awhile, but I thought maybe he had changed his mind and had decided to offer me a spot immediately since I had done so well. My dad seemed equally excited, and I could see a definite glint of excitement in his eyes as Harbaugh ran up to us. Unfortunately, however, our excitement, and our hopes for making the team, were short lived.

"Thanks for waiting," Harbaugh said. "I wanted to thank you for trying out, and Melody, you did a great job. Unfortunately, however, I don't think I'm going to be able to offer you a spot this year."

At that, I was officially crushed. To be completely honest, I felt like my heart had been torn from my chest. I had really wanted to make the team, and since I had done such a good job, I thought I had made it for sure.

And clearly I wasn't the only one. My dad's eyes narrowed and his face got red. He couldn't believe what he had just heard.

"Really? Why? She did great in the field and was one of the only girls who hit an out-of-the-parker. Actually, she hit two."

Harbaugh acknowledged the comment by nodding. "Those were some nice hits. Especially the second one. I knew it was gone the minute it left her bat. But anyway, my real concern isn't her skills. She's clearly got plenty of them, especially for a girl who's never played select ball before. My concern is her disability."

The minute he said the word 'disability' my dad's eyes got big. "What do you mean?"

"We've never had a player with a disability on the team before," Harbaugh said, "and the assistant coaches and I aren't completely confident we know how to deal with it."

At that, my dad, as had happened many times in the past when he had had to deal with similar situations, instantly got defensive.

"She doesn't have a disability," he said. "She has a special need."

Harbaugh nodded. "Call it what you will, but I'm just not certain I'm comfortable dealing with it. I'm not certain I know how."

At this point, I should probably tell you what he was talking about. I have a severe hearing impairment, and as such I cannot hear much of anything without wearing a pair of specially designed hearing aids.

"Her Little League coaches never had any issues dealing with her," my dad said.

"Good for them," Harbaugh said. "But Little League is a lot different than select ball. Things move quicker and are a lot more intense at this level. I need to be able to shout commands and have my players respond to them immediately. I don't have time to do sign language."

My dad laughed. "She doesn't do sign language. With her hearing aids on, she can hear fine. Even from her spot in center field."

"Really?" Harbaugh asked. "I didn't know that."

For a brief second, he paused, as though he was contemplating things and reevaluating his position, and I actually thought he might have a change of heart. But, much to my chagrin, his opinion didn't waiver.

"It would probably be best if she tried another team. I hear the Broncos are looking for some players. They might be willing to give her a chance."

At that, my dad (who had little patience when dealing with people like Harbaugh) clearly had heard enough.

"Fine," he said. "Thank you for your time today, Coach." He said the word 'coach' like it was venom in his mouth. "We'll contact the Broncos. But mark my words. You're going to regret this decision one day. It's just a matter of when and where."

He said it with such conviction it actually made Harbaugh's eyes get big for a second. Not knowing what else to do, he turned and, without saying anything more, jogged back to the dugout where the other coaches were waiting for him.

My dad turned to me. "Come on, Melody. Let's go."

I had barely gotten into the car, and was struggling to get my seatbelt on (the thing is such a beast at times), when I was flooded with emotion and started to cry. I just couldn't believe what had happened, nor how quickly things had changed. One minute, I thought I had made the team for sure, and the next minute I was sent packing.

My dad looked over and saw the tears running down my cheeks. He was still irritated, but now his irritation had shifted from Harbaugh to me.

"What are you doing?"

"What do you mean?" As I said it, I wiped a tear from my eye.

"Why are you crying?"

"Why wouldn't I? I just got rejected, for the third time. And for the same reason each time."

It was true. The Express tryout was the third one I had had that week, and despite doing well at each, I had been rejected by the coaches each time. The minute they found out I had a hearing impairment, they got nervous and didn't know what to do about it. And then they reacted exactly like Harbaugh. They tried to be nice, and they tried to do their best not to hurt my feelings or offend me in any way, but they cut me anyway. And they did it because they made the same mistake so many people made when they were dealing with me. They assumed that since I needed hearing aids, I needed a lot of other things, too, and as such I was going to be a burden. But it wasn't like that at all. I didn't need anything special, other than a chance. And they didn't have anything to worry about when it came to me personally. I wouldn't let them down. I knew I wasn't the best softball player in the world, and I probably never would be, but I always tried hard, and I always gave one hundred percent. In three years of Little League, I had never missed any games, and I only missed one practice and that was because I caught the flu, which was actually quite ironic since I had just gotten my flu shot the week before.

"We'll find you a team," my dad said. "You just have to be patient."

I had heard that before. After each tryout. "I've been patient. Three times now. Let's face it, dad, it's just not going to happen. Maybe I should just stick with Little League. My Little League coaches are used to dealing with me and they accept me for what I am. Maybe select ball is a bad idea."

My dad looked at me with a disappointed look on his face. "I thought you wanted to play select ball. Originally it was your idea."

I sighed. It was true, I did want to play select ball, badly, and it had indeed been my idea. "I do," I said. "But I guess some things just aren't meant to be."

At that point, as you can probably tell, I was so disappointed and so heartbroken I was contemplating giving up softball completely. Even Little League.

But my dad would hear none of it. "What are you doing?"

"What do you mean?"

"You're making excuses. And what do I always tell you about making excuses?"

I sighed. Like most dads, my dad was extremely stubborn at times, and when it came to my hearing impairment, he was even more stubborn than normal. He had refused to let me use it as an excuse, and he had always insisted that despite needing hearing aids, I could do anything I wanted as long as I was willing to work hard and never give up.

As such, I had no choice but to quote his motto, which I had heard a million times over the years. "No excuses."

"Exactly," he said. "We'll find you a team. You just have to have some faith. Eventually, we'll find a coach who will be willing to give you a chance, and then you're going to become one of the best select softball players in the state. Just you wait and see."

At that point, I wanted to believe him but I was still filled with doubt.

Without another word, he started the car, put it in gear, and we headed for home.

Fastpitch Fever
Preview

Everyone thinks being a fourteen-year-old fastpitch softball player is nothing but fun and games. Trust me, it isn't. Take today for instance. It's the final inning, and my team, the Washington Wildcats, is losing to our arch rivals, the Bellevue Beast, 4-3. We have two outs in the final inning, and it's my turn to bat. Normally, I like batting, and I'm pretty good at it, but not today. The Beast's pitcher, Nichole Williams, is really tough, and she's already struck me out twice earlier in the game. She throws several different types of pitches, and she throws them all well, but her best by far is a nasty riseball. I've never seen anyone throw a riseball as well as her. No matter how hard I try, I just can't hit it.

As I step into the batter's box, I glance quickly at the stands. My dad is sitting with the other parents in the bleachers, and he doesn't look happy. He hates it when my team loses, and he especially hates it when I strike out. If I know what's best for me, I better hit one of these riseballs, or it's going to be a long car ride home for sure.

Nichole winds up, then throws. It's just what I was dreading. Another riseball. I swing as hard as I can but I miss it by a mile.

"Strike one," blue shouts. In softball, we call the umpires blue, since they usually wear blue uniforms.

I shoot a glance at my dad. He doesn't say anything, but his face is turning red.

Nichole winds up again. This riseball is even nastier than the first. I miss it by two miles.

"Strike two," blue shouts.

"Come on, Rachel," my dad calls from the bleachers. "Keep your eyes on the ball. Keep your hands up."

I take a deep breath as I dig my cleats into the dirt. This is my last chance. If I don't hit the next pitch, I'm in deep.

The final riseball is so fast I barely see it. I miss it by three miles.

The Beast players cheer and congratulate Nichole. In the meantime, I walk back to our dugout, my head down in defeat. My coach, Ryan Taylor, greets me and tells me, "Good try," but I'm not concerned about him right now. I take my time rounding up my gear and putting it into my softball bag. I've learned from experience it's best to give my dad a few minutes to cool down after a bad game.

It's deathly silent in the car until we're half way home.

"What's the deal with riseballs?" he asks.

"I've never been able to hit riseballs," I respond. "You know that."

"But why?" he asks. "They're just like any other pitch."

"No, they're not. They start low, like a fastball, but then they go up. I always swing under them."

"So swing higher," he says.

I sigh. If only it were that simple.

"It's not that easy," I say. "I can't tell how high they're going until they get there. And then it's too late. Especially against someone like Nichole. She throws so hard."

My dad shakes his head. "It isn't that difficult, Rachel. You just need to have quick hands. Here, I'll show you."

We stop at McCall Park. McCall Park is a Little League field just a couple of blocks from our house. My dad and I practice there a lot when it isn't being used by someone else.

My dad walks to the pitching circle with a bucket of balls in one hand. We keep a bucket of balls in the trunk at all times, just for occasions like this, when he wants to teach me something. In the meantime, I take my place (somewhat hesitantly) in the batter's box.

"Hitting a riseball isn't rocket science," he says. "Just keep your eyes on the ball, as it comes in, and keep your hands up high. Don't let them drop, or you'll swing under it, just like you've been doing. Okay?"

I say okay, even though I know better. My dad and I have been through this drill hundreds of times. I've been playing softball as long as I can remember, and I've never been able to hit riseballs, no matter how hard I've tried, no matter how hard I've worked. Regardless, my dad insists he can teach me. He's extremely stubborn that way.

He throws me a riseball. I miss it by four miles.

"Rachel," he says. "Keep your eyes on the ball. Watch the ball hit the bat."

He throws me another pitch. I miss it by five miles.

"Eyes on the ball," he repeats.

He throws me another pitch. I miss it by six miles.

"Are your eyes on the ball, young lady?" he asks. He's clearly getting irritated again.

"Yes," I say as I bang my bat on the ground. He's not the only one getting irritated.

He throws me another pitch. I miss it by seven miles.

"Are you concentrating?" he asks.

"Yes," I say.

"It doesn't look like it. It looks like you're messing around. Get serious. Get ready and hit the ball. I'm not going to tell you again."

He throws another pitch. I miss it by eight miles.

"Rachel," he says as he steps out of the pitching circle. "Take that fancy bat of yours and hit the ball. Got it?"

"I'm trying," I plead.

"You're not trying hard enough. Try harder."

He throws another pitch. I miss it by nine miles.

Now he's furious. "I swear to God, Rachel, if you swing and miss once more, you're grounded for a week."

One pitch later, I'm grounded for a week.

About the Author

Jody Studdard is the author of several children's novels, including *A Different Diamond*, *Fastpitch Fever*, *Escape from Dinosaur Planet*, and *The Sheriff of Sundown City*. He is a graduate of Monroe High School (1989), the University of Washington (1993), and California Western School of Law (1995). In addition to writing, he is a practicing attorney with an office in Everett, Washington. He is a fan of the Seahawks, Storm, and Sounders FC.

Visit Jody at:

www.jstuddard.com

E-mail Jody at:

jodystuddard@jodystuddard.com

SOFTBALL STAR
books by
Jody Studdard

A Different Diamond
Fastpitch Fever
Dog in the Dugout
Missfits Fastpitch
Silence in Center

Coming Soon!

Fastpitch U

KIANA CRUISE
books by
Jody Studdard

Apocalypse

Coming Soon!

Multiplicity

Made in the USA
Charleston, SC
24 March 2014